Watching Traffic

Watching Traffic

Jane Ozkowski

Groundwood Books
House of Anansi Press
Toronto Berkeley

Published in Canada and the USA in 2016 by Groundwood Books

Groundwood Books / House of Anansi Press
groundwoodbooks.com

We acknowledge for their financial support of our publishing program the Canada
Council for the Arts, the Ontario Arts Council and the Government of Canada.

 Canada Council
for the Arts

Conseil des Arts
du Canada

 ONTARIO ARTS COUNCIL
CONSEIL DES ARTS DE L'ONTARIO
an Ontario government agency
un organisme du gouvernement de l'Ontario

With the participation of the Government of Canada
Avec la participation du gouvernement du Canada | Canada

Library and Archives Canada Cataloguing in Publication
Ozkowski, Jane, author
Watching traffic / Jane Ozkowski.
Issued in print and electronic formats.
ISBN 978-1-55498-843-3 (bound).—ISBN 978-1-55498-845-7
(html).—ISBN 978-1-55498-846-4 (mobi)
I. Title.
PS8629.Z56W38 2016   jC813'.6   C2015-908446-6
C2015-908447-4

Cover design by Michael Solomon
Cover art by Andrea Mongia

Groundwood Books is committed to protecting our natural environment. As part of our
efforts, the interior of this book is printed on paper that contains 100% post-consumer
recycled fibers, is acid-free and is processed chlorine-free.

Printed and bound in Canada

MIX
Paper from
responsible sources
FSC® C016245

1

My grandma sits on the couch beside me, and beside her are four coat hangers, a bottle of sunscreen and a mug that says *September 11th 2001*. The coffee table, side tables and mantel are all overflowing like a dollar store threw up in here.

My grandma sets a square box on my lap. It's made of stiff cardboard about the size of the pocket guide to birdwatching that's stabbing into my thigh.

"Now, Emily," she says. "I want you to have these."

I nod.

Her long hair hangs limp around her face, and her pale hands are veined like there's a blue tree growing inside her. She turned seventy-five last January, but with the light coming in lines between the closed blinds, she looks like she could be three hundred.

I open the box and squint.

"They're mine," my grandma says, and the room flips from being three-dimensional to two-dimensional to three-dimensional again.

At first I think it's the dark or the heat or the clutter that's making me see things, but then my grandma says, "Dentists only use the finest gold."

Inside the box, on top of a folded-up tissue, are six stained and broken teeth. All of them have been capped or filled with gold.

My eyes are ping-pong balls, bouncing between the teeth and my grandma, the teeth and my grandma.

My grandma nods and smiles. Her yellow dentures show between her pink lips.

I have to move a teacup, a wooden duck and three old copies of *National Geographic* before I have enough room on the coffee table to set down the teeth. I can almost smell the old plaque and crusted mashed potatoes still on them, and I try to slide the box as far away as possible.

"Thanks, Grandma."

"They were a part of me, and I want you to have them." She pushes the hair out of her face and grabs the box. She turns on the lamp on the side table and pokes the teeth around under the light. The lamp's base is made to look like a rubber boot, and its shade is in the shape of an umbrella.

"You know, Edwin, my ... your grandfather, he never let me throw anything out." She scans the room as though she'll find him hidden somewhere under the cassette tapes and ice skates or behind the pyramid of soup cans in the corner.

"I remember when we were first married I threw out a piece of old bread. He made me pull it from the garbage, cut off the mold and eat it for dinner. He was a lot older than me, you know. I got married when I was ... you're eighteen?"

I nod.

"Well, yes," she says, counting on her fingers. "I was eighteen, too. Edwin even saved the paper from the wedding presents. I think I still have it in the attic."

I'm not surprised. I'm pretty sure everything my grandma ever touched is still tucked away in this house somewhere, and when she doesn't want something anymore, she gives it to me. A few weeks ago she gave me an antique horseshoe set that weighed at least forty pounds, and the last time I was here I got a plastic bag full of animal-shaped cookie cutters. My grandma knows I work in a kitchen, and she thought it would be funny if I used them and surprised my boss.

Still, one day I might need a taxidermied trout that sings Christmas carols, or a warped mirror that makes my already wide nose look enormous and my green eyes look like old pennies.

But what am I going to do with six gold-capped teeth?

My grandma closes the box and hands it back to me.

"Like I said," she says. "Gold is precious. I had a cousin who lost a gold cup once, and he and his father traveled all over the world trying to get it back before the Nazis got to it." She picks up a one-armed doll with eyelids that open and close, and she tilts it so that it blinks at her.

"The Nazis, Grandma? I'm pretty sure that's the plot to an Indiana Jones movie." I shift on the couch and pull out a bent fork that's been jabbing my side. The whole house is gnawing into me.

"Oh," says my grandma. "Indiana Jones, I guess you're right." And her laugh is like a tidal wave that fills the whole room.

I lived with my grandma from when I was three until I was seven, and she's always been like this. Sometimes for dinner we'd sit on the kitchen floor and eat with our hands. We'd have dry cereal, mushrooms, scrambled eggs and maybe a bowl of ice cubes, and my grandma would tell me we were eating like this because I was a feral child used to foraging.

"I was walking through the woods one day," she'd say, "and I heard this odd little chirp, not quite like a bird. I followed the sound, and there you were, a tiny baby covered in dirt, eating mushrooms just like this off a tree stump." She'd hold up a mushroom and look at it like inside there really was a forest and a baby …

I check the time on my phone and slide the box of teeth back onto the coffee table. They'll probably get swallowed in the tornado that is my grandma's house, and maybe she'll forget she even gave them to me.

"I have to go to work," I tell her and kiss her on the cheek.

I'm almost out the door, home free, but her voice is a hook pulling me back.

"Emily, don't forget these." And she waves the little box at me like today will be the day I really need six gold-capped teeth, and I'll be glad I took them with me.

The mid-August sun isn't much of a relief from my grandma's living room as I head toward the central overpass and my job in West Cavanaugh. It's so bright I have to walk with my eyes closed and one foot on the grass so I don't step off the sidewalk into traffic.

I'm still walking blind when I hear a sound like an air conditioner clearing its throat, and I open my eyes just in time to stop myself from walking directly into Mrs. Mack.

"Emily, hi," she says. "Do you have something in your eye?" Technically she's a woman, but she's got a thick neck and tiny eyes, and I have a feeling she might be thirty to forty percent otter.

"Oh hi, Mrs. Mack. Yes, it's just dust or something." I blink my eyes to make it look authentic, then shift my bag to the other shoulder and try to look smart and busy and not like I'm wandering the streets carrying a box of human teeth.

When I was in elementary school, Mrs. Mack would volunteer in my class a few times a week. Her older daughter was a competitive figure skater, and Mrs. Mack spent so much time at the rink that she had to come to the school to remember what her son Kyle looked like.

"It's funny I should run into you," she says. "I was talking to Kyle about you the other day." She fluffs up her otter hair while she speaks. "I was saying what an accomplishment it is that you graduated high school with the rest of your class. Kyle has had every advantage in the world, and he barely made it. To think you did it with all the adversity you've had to overcome."

"Why wouldn't I graduate?"

"Exactly, Emily. That's the right attitude. You can do anything you put your mind to. I truly believe that, especially for you." And I'm pulled into a baby-powder-scented hug. The box of teeth rattles as we break apart, and I try to arrange my face so that I look like a mature adult human being.

When she used to volunteer at my school, Mrs. Mack would sit in one of the little plastic chairs beside me at the back of the class, and I would pretend I was a super genius trapped in a clinic and being tested to understand how I'd become so smart and powerful. Mrs. Mack was the evil scientist, and I wrote each of the words in my notebook backward so she wouldn't figure out my tricks.

Mrs. Mack never believed me when I told her I knew how to write the words the right way.

"There's no shame in not knowing, Emily, but there is shame in lying," she'd say, and she'd give me this look like when you watch a video of a puppy with its head stuck in a box.

Mrs. Mack clamps me on the shoulders and looks deep into my eyes like she's about to tell me an ancient family secret.

"You know, Emily," she finally says. "I was talking with some of the other parents at graduation, and we were all saying how proud we are of you. I heard you're not moving away to school or to travel like most of the other kids, but you've done great. More than great. I like to think this whole town had a hand in raising you, and you've blossomed into a beautiful young woman."

I should have brought a snack and maybe a carrier pigeon to send a message back home. I could be trapped here forever.

"I know your poor mother's not around to see you," she continues. "But I can tell you she'd be just as proud of you as we all are." And she throws herself into another hug. Her hot little otter hands knead into my back, and she makes a sound in the back of her throat like she's trying to sing in whale language.

I think what freaks people out most about my mother's death is that when the maid or whoever came to clean the shitty motel room my mother and I were staying in, I was covered in blood. It's not just that it was a suicide or that I was the one who found her, but that in the middle of everything, I somehow got covered in blood.

It was fifteen years ago, but it's like absolutely nothing interesting has happened in Cavanaugh since then. In junior high, kids called me Suicide Baby, and even now I keep thinking

I should rob a bank or light a church on fire, because every time anyone looks at me they still see a three-year-old covered in blood, all alone in some dingy washroom at the edge of town.

"Mrs. Mack," I try to say over the whale music. "Mrs. Mack, listen, it was really nice running into you, but I have to go. I have to go to work."

She sounds out a few more notes before she finally sets me free, and I have to walk triple speed over the overpass to make it to work on time.

2

Today is my friend Lincoln's last day at work. He slices flour and butter together while I sprinkle more flour across the long metal table.

I'm pretty sure this basement was a morgue before it became the headquarters for Pamela's Country Catering for All Occasions. Pamela gave the body-examining table a good scrub and shoved an oven in the corner, and we've been making egg salad, tuna salad and chicken salad sandwiches down here ever since.

"Today we're making horse penis tarts for the holidays," Lincoln says to an imaginary camera. "Try not to handle the dough too much. If you let the butter melt, the pastry won't be flaky."

Pamela is away today, and Lincoln is wearing his hairnet like a crown over his rough blond hair. Our friend Melissa's supposed to be here, too, but she's late, of course.

"Now we'll take some questions from our studio audience," Lincoln says. He scans the kitchen as though it's full of people, and I wave my hand through the air, making it snow flour back onto the table.

"Yes," he says. "You, in the striped shirt."

"Well, hello," I say in my best southern accent. "First of all, I just want to say that I *love* the show. Your assistant Emily Robinson is so beautiful."

"Good looking," Lincoln nods. "But a few cents short of a nickel." And he taps his temple.

I flick a piece of pastry dough at him. "Well, I was wondering if you could suggest a spice I could put in these tarts to hide the taste of rat poison."

"A common problem. The trick with poison is that you don't want to conceal the taste so much as compliment it."

But then Melissa finally arrives, and the cameras dissolve.

"Your Majesty," I say. "So kind of you to come to our lowly kitchen."

I bow and Lincoln bows, and Melissa pushes the hair out of her face. She's wearing cutoffs and an oversized black T-shirt. She hangs up a tote bag big enough to hold three to four mid-sized tortoises, which reminds me of the three-quarters-full bottle of whiskey at the bottom of my bag.

"A little last-day celebration?" I ask Lincoln, pulling it out. The bottle is a pendulum between him and Melissa.

Lincoln groans.

"Why do you always have to get whiskey?"

"We're in training to be badasses," I tell him. "We can only drink straight whiskey and black coffee, and we can never sleep."

Melissa takes the bottle and leans her head back to drink. The knuckles of her right hand are bruised and cut up.

"Shit," says Lincoln. "What happened to your hand?"

Melissa screws the lid back on the bottle and sets it sideways on the table. I watch her mangled hand on top as she spins the whiskey, trying to decide who to kiss.

"Dan and I got into a fight," she says.

"And you punched him?" I ask. The bruises are stains on the inside of her skin.

"No, I punched a tree and then the overpass."

"Of course you did," says Lincoln.

"And then you punched a baby and an old man with one leg," I add.

"Yeah," she says. "Something like that."

I imagine Melissa and her boyfriend Dan on the southern overpass. It's dark, and cars speed below on the highway that slices Cavanaugh in two. Melissa shouts into the wind, and her long brown hair flies around her head like she's been electrocuted. She punches the concrete that separates her from a drop into traffic. Her hand is bleeding, but the next time she punches, the concrete breaks instead of her bones ...

Melissa and I have been best friends since grade two. When it somehow came out that I left class once a week to meet with a counselor because of what my mother did, and Melissa left class once a week to meet with a counselor because of her anger problems, none of the other kids wanted to play with us. So we decided we would only be friends with each other.

We were born two weeks apart, and we used to tell everyone we were twins. Through most of high school we had this plan that when we graduated we'd open up a coffee shop called Gemini Luncheonette. The seats would be hammock swings, and we'd project weird old movies on the walls.

"Did you get this from my brother?" Melissa asks, taking up the whiskey again.

"What?" says Lincoln. "I asked Robert to pick me up a case of beer a few days ago, and he said something about people being ungrateful and how he's closing down the business."

"You're missing my charm and my good looks," I tell him, taking a swig from the bottle.

Melissa's brother Robert is two years older than us. He just got a job on the graveyard shift at the new twenty-four-hour grocery store in town, but before that he made most of his money helping with his cousin's moving business and selling alcohol to underage kids at a twenty-five percent markup.

Lincoln sniffs the whiskey and pulls back like a tiny fist in there just punched him in the face.

"I can't drink this straight."

"You could mix it with milk or applesauce," Melissa says with the fridge open.

"Here, baby." I fill a tablespoon with whiskey and airplane it toward his mouth. "Take your medicine."

He drinks but refuses any more.

"How are you going to survive in the outback if you don't know how to drink?" Melissa asks. Lincoln and I are cutting pastry circles for the butter tarts while she starts on the filling.

"You know Australia's more than deserts and shit. They have actual cities."

"Still," I say. "We need to prepare you for anything." I come at him with the spoon again, but he swats my hand away, splashing whiskey down the front of his shirt.

"Stop," he says. "I'm as prepared as I can be. I still can't believe I'm leaving in eight days. Tomorrow is my last full Sunday in Canada."

Lincoln has been talking about getting out of Cavanaugh since we started hanging out two years ago. There's a highway that cuts the town in two, and he thinks if he follows it, it will lead him to a magical kingdom full of travelers who read Sartre and speak Japanese. I think the first thing he ever said to me was, "Have you ever noticed that this whole town smells like ham?"

"And I'm leaving for Halifax in less than two weeks," says Melissa. "It feels like this summer just started, but pretty soon we'll all be gone."

"Not everyone," says Lincoln. He's rolling the leftover dough out again to make more circles.

"Someone has to keep an eye on things around here," I tell them.

I got accepted into the community college two towns over from Cavanaugh, but I don't even know what Communications is or why I would want to study it. My forms and registration papers were due over a month ago. I was hoping they would fill themselves out, but they didn't.

I lean against the warm oven and watch Lincoln and Melissa work. They're on a television show, and this is the last episode of the last season. The set is tired and the actors are getting old. Soon the screen will fade and I'll be left alone on my living-room couch staring at static.

"Are you going to help or what?" asks Melissa.

"Considering it's Lincoln's last day," I say. "Really, we should let him do everything."

By the end of the day Melissa and I are sitting on the metal table in the center of the room. We swing our feet while

Lincoln tries to clean around us. We pass the whiskey back and forth, and Melissa DJs, spinning the dial on the scratchy radio from pop songs to what sound like Latvian Christmas carols without ever staying on a station for more than a minute.

"Come on, guys," Lincoln says. "The sooner we get this done, the sooner we can leave."

"This is the last time you get to wipe down this table and put these bowls away," I say. "We couldn't possibly take this moment away from you."

"Savor this," Melissa tells him. "This is the end of the best years of your life."

When Lincoln finally finishes, he leaves his truck in Pamela's driveway, and the three of us walk to the southern overpass to watch the earth swallow the sun. The cars drive back and forth on the black line below, and none of the drivers looks up to see us standing on the overpass and the sky leaking pink and yellow and red over everything.

Before I was born, before the mall and the movie theater, the highway used to be the main street in Cavanaugh. As the town got bigger, though, so did the highway — first two lanes, then four — with Cavanaugh bursting around it. People coming from Toronto two hours away didn't want to slow down for local traffic on their way to cottages and ski resorts farther north, so they tore down all the shops and turned the main street into a proper highway with three bridges going over top.

Melissa pulls out her phone to send a text, and the sky is a Technicolor Dreamcoat above us.

"I'd better go," she says. "I have to meet up with Dan."

"What?" I ask. "I thought we were supposed to hang out."

Melissa looks at her bruised hand, and I scan the concrete edge of the overpass to see if there's a dent from where she punched.

"Well, I … we did hang out … all afternoon." She turns to look at the cars driving under us.

"You were supposed to cut my hair," I say, but she's deaf to it. All summer Dan has been a magnet, and she's had a metal plate where her head should be.

She keeps her eyes on the cars, and Lincoln sweeps his arms around both of us. He presses us into the railing of the overpass and starts to sing, *"Oh Danny boy, the pipes, the pipes are calling …"*

Warm wind pushes the hair back from our faces. Melissa is still turned away, but with Lincoln's arm around me, I can feel his voice reverberate through him like inside his chest there is a great lake.

"The summer's gone and all the flowers are dying …" He doesn't hit all the notes, but his voice is deep and clear, and the song goes on and on. The melody is carried by the highway, out of Cavanaugh and away from us.

"If you'll not fail to tell me that you love me, I'll simply sleep in peace until you come to me."

When Lincoln finishes, the three of us look around like we're not sure who we are or how we got here. The sun has set now. There's just a light blue line on the horizon and the town with all its lights on.

"That was nice," Melissa says. She pats Lincoln on the cheek and spits over the overpass because her body is sixty percent water and she can't keep it in anymore.

"How about tomorrow?" she asks me. "Come over before Neil's party."

— 22 —

"You've been flaking on me all summer," I say, and I would say more if Lincoln's arm wasn't still around me with his hand sneaking up to tickle my armpit. I laugh and hit him away before turning back to Melissa.

"Fine," I tell her.

She pats me on the cheek, too, and kicks a rock in front of her as she goes, as though trying to prove that even though she got a huge scholarship to go to her dream school she's still a troubled teen with anger issues, and no one would dare mess with her.

With Melissa's next kick, the rock goes off course and lands in the middle of the overpass. She walks on without it, her hair a dark mane around her head, and her body nothing more than a silhouette under a streetlight.

And then it's Lincoln and me looking out at the highway. Its long black tongue swallows the cars into infinity, and eight days from today, Lincoln will be swallowed, too, upside down on the exact other side of the earth.

"I don't feel like going home," he says.

"Good," I say.

"But what are we going to do?"

When I go to pull out the whiskey, I hit against something hard and flat. It's half out of my bag before I realize it's the box my grandma gave me. I tuck it away and go for the alcohol instead.

"Here," I tell Lincoln. "Drink this."

"I can't. I drove. Remember?"

"I'll drive." I take a sip from the bottle and spray whiskey out of my mouth and over the overpass. Now all the cars are going to be drunk and crash into each other in a spectacular fiery mess.

"Oh, thanks. That's helpful."

"Take your truck to my house and we'll get drunk there."

"How will I get home?" He pats down his hair, which always looks like it's growing in backward.

"Stay over."

"What about your dad?"

"It's okay. He was lobotomized years ago. He barely recognizes me anymore."

"Emily."

I start jogging away from Lincoln toward Pamela's and his truck. The teeth rattle against the top of the box as I run. They're trying to eat their way out.

"In a few days I may never see you ever again," I call. "You have to get drunk with me. It's your duty."

"Emily? Maybe it's that you're probably drunk, but are you okay?" Lincoln asks when we're in his truck driving to my house. "Like with us all leaving?"

It's always been like this. I'll be at the post office picking up stamps for my grandma or getting fries from the fry truck behind the mall, and people I barely know will come up to me and say, "Emily, it's so nice to see you. How are you? How are you *really*?" Like there's a danger I'm going to transform into a spaceship or shoot blood out my eyes just because of something my mother did when I was almost too young to remember.

There's nothing wrong with me, though. This is just how I act.

The light from the streetlight makes the line in Lincoln's bum chin more defined. I imagine a little fart coming out of it.

"Yeah, I'm fine," I tell him. "But thanks for asking."

When we get to my house, my dad is in the basement watching a documentary on killer whales.

"Lincoln's going to sleep over, okay?" I call to him.

He squints at me standing at the top of the stairs like he's looking at me through scuba goggles from the bottom of the ocean.

"Lincoln," he says. I'm not sure if it's a question.

"You've met him before."

Lincoln comes beside me on the stairs and waves.

"Oh, okay, hello, yes, okay," says my dad.

We pour whiskey into cups of lemonade and go to the computer in my dad's office. Lincoln spins the propeller on a replica of the first biplane while we watch videos of old men getting puppies as presents.

And when my dad goes to bed, we watch porn in the basement on the lowest volume.

"This is gross," I say. "Why do we always watch this?"

It's a video called *Atlantic Adventure, Nurses at Sea* that Lincoln got me for my birthday in June. We've watched it three times already.

"Because it's gross."

"Oh, of course," I say. The captain takes three nurses under the deck to show them how the pistons are lubricated.

"Are most penises that big? I haven't seen a lot of penises, but the ones I've seen didn't look like that."

"I don't know," says Lincoln. "The screen is just a penis. There's nothing to give it perspective."

Later, someone takes my bed and drops it into the ocean. The cars from the highway are waves, and we're just a lifeboat with water in every direction. I turn my back to Lincoln and he scoops me up so that we're spooning. An ambulance siren comes through the open window, and I imagine its lights flashing across the inside of my skull and turning my thoughts blue and red.

"Why do you have to go to Australia?" I ask.

"Well," he says. He loosens his grip and sighs into the darkness. "There's a whole world out there. I just want to, like, see everything and do everything and experience everything. Don't you?"

"I don't even know where Australia is."

His left arm is flopped across me. It presses me into the mattress, and stuffing and springs come out my mouth.

"Stay here and we'll get married," I say, and Lincoln laughs.

"Remember the date we tried to go on when we met? Do you really want a whole lifetime of that?"

"It could be a sexless marriage."

His hand roams my face until it covers my mouth.

"Is it because my dowry's not big enough?" I manage to get out.

"You are so annoying sometimes," he says, and we lie there listening to crickets and the highway and my dad snoring in the other room.

My grandma used to tell me that crickets are immortal. They're old people who were allowed to live forever but not be young forever. Their bodies kept getting older until they became so frail that their bones folded up. All that's left of them now are paperclip bodies and voices no one understands. One day their bodies will dissolve and their voices will become the wind.

"Emily?" Lincoln's voice sounds like it's coming from another country. "I know this is supposed to be this really exciting time and everything, and I am excited, but I'm also really scared to move away."

I flip around so that I'm facing him. The neighbors have their back light on, and half of Lincoln's face is gold.

"I spent all my money on my plane ticket, and I told everyone how I'm going and how I'm never going to come back to Cavanaugh, but what if I don't like it?" When he concentrates, his eyebrows almost touch and his lips pout out. He looks at me with his face frozen like that, as though he's a gold statue of himself.

"I don't know," I say. "I don't think you can know."

He sighs and puts his hand to his face like he's checking to make sure his features can still move.

"It still doesn't feel real that I'm going," he says. "I can see myself getting off the plane, and I've got a place to stay for the first two nights, but then what?"

"Then you'll be living in Australia," I say.

"Then I'll be living in Australia." He puts his arm around me and pulls me into him.

"Maybe I should just stay here," he says. "Maybe we should all just stay here." And then he kisses me, big and wet and whiskey, and it almost seems like the right thing to do right now, but ...

I pull away and so does he.

The laugh starts as a giggle but grows because my blood's been carbonated. I have to put a pillow over my face so I don't wake my dad. Lincoln starts laughing, too, and we laugh until we can't breathe. I feel less drunk, but I feel like I might be high.

"What?" I say while I'm still trying to catch my breath. "Why did you do that?"

"I don't know," Lincoln says, and we laugh again.

"Maybe we should just go to sleep," he says.

"Good idea."

We roll over again so that Lincoln is the baby spoon and I've got my arms around him. My bag is at the foot of my bed with the box of old gold teeth still in it, and the tree in my backyard shifts in the wind, making the neighbor's back light flicker like the house is in flames.

3

Lincoln leaves early, but I stay in bed until after noon. I lie with my feet on my pillow and my head where my feet would normally go so that more blood will get to my brain and my dreams will be more vivid.

Neil is having a party tonight, but that's not until eight, and I know that halfway through the party I'll be waiting for it to be over so I can go home. All through high school I was waiting to graduate so I could start my adult life, and now that high school is over I'm waiting for something to happen so I can figure out what I'm supposed to be doing.

When I do make it out of bed, my dad is in the kitchen heating a can of brown beans on the stove.

"Good morning," he says. "Do you want some beans?" He used to have hair, but he's almost completely bald now. He's six-foot-four, and when I first met him I remember thinking he was the tallest person I'd ever seen.

"It's okay," I say. "I'll probably just have peanut butter."

"You always have peanut butter."

"It's what I like."

He brings his bowl to the table and flips through the paper with one hand. The sports section falls to the floor. It's a bird that's been shot.

"I've got that conference in Montreal in a few weeks," he says. "I was thinking you could come with me if you wanted." Behind him the sound of cars on the highway drives through the open window.

"What would I do there?" I ask.

He pats his pockets looking for a pen for the crossword and then runs his fingers across his scalp like his hand forgot he doesn't have hair.

"We could go to the Biodome again. Didn't we do that? When did we go?"

"Yeah we did," I say. "I think I was ten."

He's got his pen in one hand and a spoonful of beans in the other. He looks between the two and then back at me.

"Really? I thought it was only a few years ago."

I shrug.

"There are some good schools there, too," he tells me with his face back to the paper. "Maybe we could set up a tour at a culinary school or else for Small Business Management." He counts the letters of a word on his fingers, and his face creases like the paper in front of him.

"Small Business Management?" I ask.

"For that café, Twin Bistro, or whatever you and Melissa are going to call it." His eyes are still on the paper, and there's a blue ink mark on his lip like he accidentally brought his pen to his mouth instead of his spoon.

When he was younger, he studied marine biology. He went back to school a few years later to become an environmental consultant, but I sometimes feel like part of him is still underwater.

"Gemini Luncheonette?" I ask.

He nods.

"That's not happening anymore. All Melissa can talk about is getting out of here as fast as possible. I'll probably barely see her after she leaves." I get a piece of bread and spread peanut butter across it.

My dad watches me like he's waiting for my words to be translated to Morse code, sent to his submarine and then put back into English.

"I don't know about that. She's only going to … to where?"

"To Halifax, Dad."

"Oh, right. That's quite far." He's still holding his loaded spoon in his left hand, and one of the beans jumps overboard and lands on the paper.

Even after eleven years of living with my dad, I still sometimes feel like we speak different languages. When I was seven and first moved in with him, I spent most of my time watching him the way the animals in their cages watch the tourists at the zoo. He woke me up at the same time every morning and set out cereal and milk. While I ate, he'd say things like, "The landlord said he'd fix this cabinet before we moved in, but he hasn't yet." Or else, "I got Oreos for your lunch. Do you like Oreos? There are oatmeal cookies, too, or I can pick up something else." He was so tall, he seemed to go all the way up to the ceiling, and I was sure his legs were made of tree trunks.

Compared to my grandma's house with her wooden shoe collection and the boxes of Christmas decorations stacked in the hallway all year round, this rented house with nothing in it but the sound of the highway felt like it was wrapped in plastic with the air sucked out.

My grandma had gotten me to school on time every morning, but sometimes I wore a Halloween costume or a dress over pants, and my lunch was three hotdogs in a thermos, buns and a full bottle of ketchup …

"Maybe you could move there, too," my dad says after so long I can hardly remember what we were talking about.

"What, to Halifax? Melissa can barely make time for me here in Cavanaugh."

"Right," he says. "Leave it with me." As though this is the same sort of problem as where to install drainage pipes so that building a shopping mall on a marsh won't disrupt the waterfowl.

I'm pretty sure my dad only has one friend, Clem. Every few weeks they get together to go fishing or else to get drunk and argue about the mating habits of sea slugs. In grade seven, when I told my dad I was being bullied by some of the girls at school, he enrolled me in clarinet lessons with the idea that if people knew I could play an instrument they would think I was cool and stop picking on me.

"I went to see Grandma yesterday," I say before my dad decides to fix my problems by signing me up for traditional Irish dancing or gnome painting.

"Did she give you anything?"

He knows about the other things — the T-shirt with two cats holding hands and *I Heart Florida* written in glitter, the globe so old it's still got the USSR on it, the sandwich bag of old stamps steamed off of envelopes. It used to be funny. My dad probably still thinks it's funny. He thinks Monty

Python and commercials with talking animals are funny.

"Not this time," I say.

In my room, I take the box of teeth out of my bag, but I don't open it. Every year at Christmas and on my birthday, my dad's side of the family in Alberta sends me candles or purple scarves or body lotion with sparkles in it, and I always end up giving everything away, usually to Melissa's cousin Darlene who likes that kind of thing.

It's just that my grandma in Cavanaugh always seems so excited when she gives me something. I've still got the set of cutlery she told me the queen of England used to use.

According to my grandma, the queen was an old friend of my grandfather's family. Her Majesty used to fly over for brunch sometimes, and they had a set of forks and knives especially for her. My grandfather inherited the cutlery, and my grandma passed it along to me.

Of course there's no way any of that could be true. My grandfather's father was a failed minister in a town so small it doesn't even exist anymore, and I think his father was a farmer, but at least the story is good.

Meanwhile, this is a box of worn-out teeth. Yes, gold is valuable, but if I keep these, I'll probably end up on a daytime talk show special, the ones where the host goes into a woman's house and finds her wading through McDonald's wrappers and broken toasters four feet deep. The woman thinks her husband has died somewhere in the back room, but the house is too full of junk to find the body.

On the other side of Cavanaugh, past a street where half the houses have windows made of cardboard and tape, three pawnshops stand like old saloons. All of them have signs in their windows that say *Cash 4 Gold*.

It's hard to decide from the street which pawnshop to go into, so I pick the one with the bicycle in the window. A bell rings when I open the door, and the whole shop smells like the inside of a dog's mouth.

There's a shelf of old clocks to my right. I slide my fingers along the top until they hit something sticky. Probably the blood of a virgin or a centaur.

"Hey," someone says at the back of the shop. He has thick brown hair in a ponytail like a rope down his back. He's tall, muscular and surprisingly hot for a guy who works in a pawnshop. He's probably an undercover cop trying to mingle with the Cavanaugh lowlife.

He doesn't look that much older than me, though. He must be very ambitious to be an undercover cop at eighteen or twenty. I wish I was that motivated.

"Hi," I say. I was expecting a retired pirate or an almost reformed alcoholic, but this guy looks cool. His T-shirt is probably for an obscure band I've never heard of, and he has a tattoo of a pine tree on his left forearm.

"Do you guys take these?" I slide the box across the counter.

I should have put on mascara or something. I bite my lips so they'll look red and tilt my head forward and to the right like Melissa taught me so my nose doesn't look so enormous.

The guy opens the box and looks down at the teeth, then back at me, the teeth and then me. The corners of his mouth edge toward each other in a frown.

"What the fuck?" he finally says, and then he smiles. One side of his mouth is overly enthusiastic, and it goes up more than the other. The guy's lips are thin, and maybe one side of his face is trying to compensate.

"I'm not supposed to ask," he says. "But where did these come from?"

"I just punched this guy mouth." I say. *Stupid, stupid, stupid.* "I mean, I just punched this guy out, right in the mouth, and then I stole his teeth."

"Oh, yeah?"

It's then that I notice someone's trapped a rhythm in my finger, and I'm tapping it out on the counter as quickly as I can. When I touched that centaur blood my hands must have gotten cursed. They control themselves now. One of my wild hands climbs my collarbone to my throat and starts to strangle me.

I can't breathe. What's happening to me?

One of the pawnshop guy's eyebrows slides up his face and he leans back a little. He knows about my cursed hands.

I shove my hands into my back pockets, and the guy looks down at the box.

"We'll take the gold, I guess, but you've gotta get the teeth off first." He puts the lid back on and slides the box across the counter using just his pointer finger.

My bag gets caught on the handlebar of a bicycle on the way out, and I'm jerked backward then forward onto the hot pavement outside the pawnshop. The box with the teeth escapes and lands at the feet of a woman with a baby carriage.

"Here," she says, handing me the box.

Keep it. It's a gift for your baby, I almost tell her, just so I can watch her discover the teeth and scream. I'm already a deranged creature who goes into pawnshops and tries to sell teeth to hot guys.

Instead I thank her, shove the teeth into the bottom of my bag and continue to walk with my legs feeling too short or too long or else like there are too many of them.

I stash the teeth at my house for Future Emily to deal with and borrow some beers from my dad before heading to Melissa's three streets over.

Melissa stands barefoot on her front porch with her lip in her mouth. Her black tank top slides off her shoulder, and her hair zigzags off her head. She drums her fingers on the railing, and the cuts on her knuckles catch in the light.

"Yo," she says and makes a peace sign.

I laugh at her and walk past to kick my shoes off in the front hallway.

"I made lemonade," she says. She sets my shoes on the shoe rack in the closet beside the other neatly lined pairs and follows me into the kitchen. "And there's some kind of juice, too." She takes a container of red liquid out of the fridge and drinks from it. It leaves a red smile above her lip, and she wipes it with the back of her arm.

"I think it's cherry," she says.

I tell her I'm good with lemonade.

The ice cubes are shaped like hearts, and the trim around the tops of the glasses is the exact same green as the walls. Melissa spills a drip of lemonade on the counter but wipes it up immediately before sitting across from me at the table with a pair of scissors between us.

"You've had those scissors forever," I tell her. The handles are orange plastic, and there's a square of tape stuck to the top blade.

Melissa scratches off the tape and runs her thumb across the blade, testing for sharpness.

"Maybe," she says.

"I remember being, like, eight years old, and your mom using them to make a chain of paper dolls for us. I thought she was a magician. I went home and asked my dad to make some for me, but we just ended up with little paper triangles all over the floor."

Melissa nods, but she's hardly paying attention. She scratches her shoulder with one hand, and with the other she uses the scissors to snip the air like she's trying to cut me away. Her eyes are large and brown and shine in the light reflecting off the blade.

"Hey," I say. "You're not still ... you're okay, right?"

"Yeah, of course."

And the scissors go crashing back to the table. They leave the smallest scratch in the wood that Melissa tries to rub out with her thumb before turning to me.

"I don't ... I don't do that anymore," she says, and then disappears down the hall for a towel and a brush.

When Melissa comes back, her eyes go up and down my body. I'm sitting on one of the wooden chairs in the middle of the kitchen. I've taken my shirt off so it doesn't get covered in hair.

"What are you doing?" she asks.

"No one's home, right?"

"My parents are at their friends' cottage, and Robert's doing some video game thing with Mark, but you don't have to ..." She holds up the towel. "I can just cover you."

"It's okay. It's been an odd twenty-four hours. The last thing I need is to go to Neil's and be the girl covered in little bits of hair."

Melissa's eyes are still on my shirt on the floor.

"Why? What else happened?" She picks up the shirt and folds it before setting it on the table.

"Well, first off my grandma gave me this messed-up gift — way weirder than any of the others. I tried to pawn it, but I didn't know how and ended up looking like a huge loser in front of this hot guy who worked at the pawnshop."

"Sure," she says. She's at the sink facing the open window with her hair blown behind her back and the sound of the highway getting in.

"And last night, Lincoln tried to kiss me."

"What?" she asks. She pushes her hair back and turns to look at me, maybe for the first time today.

"Well, he did kiss me. We were drunk, and we just kind of kissed."

"What does that mean?"

"Nothing. It was just one of those funny moments that happens sometimes."

Melissa leans against the sink and studies the fraying edge of her tank top. Her bottom lip is between her teeth, and her eyebrows furrow together.

"I think I've made out with almost all of our friends now," I tell her.

She turns back to the sink and runs the tap until the water's warm enough to wet my hair under.

"You haven't made out with me," she says.

"Well, come here." I purse my lips and head toward her, but she dodges me, and I stick my head under the tap.

"I'm just going to give you a trim," Melissa tells me after combing out my hair and wrapping the towel around my shoulders. "I was thinking you'd look good with bangs, but maybe we should leave it for now."

"What am I going to do when I have to pay for haircuts?" I ask.

"You do have to pay. It's forty bucks or a pint of blood."

"Okay. Cut me right here." I point to my neck, and she holds the cold blade against it. Metal, flesh, metal, flesh, and the scissors warm on my skin.

"Emily?" Melissa says. She takes the scissors away and takes a deep breath like the air is heavy. "Listen."

A warm breeze blows through the kitchen and stirs the receipts magnetized to the fridge.

"I don't hear anything." I tell her.

"That's not what I …"

"Well, what?"

But she picks up the scissors and goes at my hair. The blades flap like the wings of a mechanical canary.

"Shit," Melissa mutters to herself, but her hands are still flying.

"What happened?" I ask. I grab at my hair to see if she's given me a bald patch, but she brushes my hand away.

"It's fine," she says. "It's nothing."

She turns the radio on loud. The sound comes scratchy out of the speakers like the kitchen has suddenly filled with bats, and Melissa's hands flap around my head. Bits of dark hair fly everywhere, and the voice of a used-car salesman bashes itself against the appliances.

"God, what's wrong with you today?" I ask, but I don't know if Melissa can hear me over the music and the scissors and bats dive-bombing our heads.

When Melissa finishes, I go to the bathroom to look at my reflection. My hair looks exactly the same, only wetter and shorter.

"It looks good," I call down the hall, but I don't hear anything back. The radio is still blasting in the kitchen, and the next-door neighbors are mowing their lawn.

The first time Melissa cut my hair we were thirteen. Her parents were at one of Robert's hockey games, and we had the house to ourselves to make triple-chocolate brownies and steal sips from her parents' liquor cabinet.

It took Melissa over an hour to give me a trim. She measured out the pieces carefully and cut almost one hair at a time. When she was finished, we stood in the bathroom together and looked at the layers spilling over my shoulders.

"Whoa," I said.

She stood behind me with her lip in her mouth and adjusted a few loose hairs around my face.

"Here," she said. She was still taller than me then, and she pressed on my shoulders so I was crouching with her stomach to my back. She smelled like watermelon shampoo and gin as she combed her curly hair over my straight hair, and our hair ran together like two rivers.

I could only see half my face in the mirror, my green eyes with Melissa's hair on top, and something about the person reflected back seemed like a total stranger. Melissa's body was warm against mine like she was a part of me. She put her palm on my cheek, and my fingers tingled like it was my hand feeling my face and not hers. I put my hand on my other cheek and then on top of her hand, but she pulled away and pushed the hair back from her eyes.

"You should wash those bits of hair off or they'll itch," she said, and she disappeared down the hall ...

I find Melissa in the kitchen stabbing a box of crackers with the scissors she used to cut my hair. Crumbs and bits of paper spill across the table like the crackers got hit by a meteorite.

"The box wouldn't open," she says. She sweeps the crumbs into the sink and wipes down the table before pulling a bottle of vodka from the freezer. "Let's get drunk now."

"Seriously?" I ask. The clock on the microwave says it's 4:52. The party isn't for three hours.

"Let's get really fucked up tonight. We've barely drunk together all summer."

"And whose fault is that?" I ask, but she's already pouring the vodka into what's left of our lemonade. "Can't we just hang out like we're normal people?"

"But we're not normal people." She drops a heart-shaped ice cube into my glass and forces it into my hand.

While everyone else was at choir practice or on the soccer team, Melissa and I spent the first half of high school lighting fires in the forest at the edge of Cavanaugh or else standing on opposite overpasses and yelling swear words at each other over the highway. Melissa's gotten pretty serious about school in the last few years, but she still likes to hold onto her image as this rebellious outcast no one understands.

We take our drinks to the front porch, but Melissa can't keep still. She finishes her vodka in three sips, then walks barefoot across her driveway, wincing at the heat of the black pavement baked in the sun all day.

"Remember doing this when we were little?" she calls. "We'd pretend we were walking on hot coals and see who could stand it the longest."

"Of course," I say.

But when I go to join her, she steps onto the grass and asks, "Want to do shots? I think I'm going to do a shot."

I shake my head, and she disappears into the kitchen without me.

By the time we leave for Neil's party, Melissa is walking like her legs are made of drinking straws. We have to stop at the southern overpass and watch the cars go by for a few minutes while she regains her strength.

"I'm sorry," she says. "I had to drink this much, for courage."

"What are you talking about?" I ask.

"Okay," Melissa says. "Okay." She looks at her cut-up hand, then presses it into the concrete edge of the overpass. I'm afraid she's going to try to punch it again, but instead she takes off running.

I let her go ahead of me but keep an eye on her in case she loses her balance and falls into the path of oncoming traffic.

4

Neil's whole neighborhood has a wall around it to stop the sound of the highway from getting in. His parents have a cottage in Muskoka, and they've been there most of the summer, which means we've been having parties at his house most of the summer.

When Melissa and I get there, we walk in without knocking and follow the voices to the basement. It's the kind of house that could be nice if the carpet was a lighter shade of green, there were fewer bowls of potpourri and you took down all the pictures of Jesus. We pass by a group of kids who took advanced math and science and only talk to each other playing a drinking game in the laundry room and enter the main room in the basement, which was refinished a few years ago. It's got a pool table, brown couches with animal print accent pillows and a tank of goldfish in the corner.

Neil is already drunk and high. He's got a mustache made of painter's tape, and he's arguing with Melissa's boyfriend Dan about internet privacy or something like that. Melissa wobbles toward them and drapes her body on top of Dan's, but she turns her cheek when he goes to kiss her.

Lincoln and Mark are playing pool with Melissa's cousin Darlene. I sit on the arm of the couch to watch and open one of the beers I borrowed from my dad.

"I've been to IKEA three times," Darlene is saying. "I don't even know if I'll be able to fit all the stuff I got into my dorm room."

"That's the thing," says Mark, chalking his pool cue. "I don't want to get a whole bunch of stuff and then find out I don't need it. I don't even know what kind of person I'm going to be in university. Ideally I wouldn't even bring clothes because I might not even dress the same."

"You should at least bring a change of underwear," says Darlene. "And maybe sheets."

Mark hits the white ball across the table. It goes directly between the red and purple balls and doesn't hit anything. He smirks at me and turns back to Darlene.

"Well, I will bring clothes," he says. "I don't actually have enough money to buy all new stuff, but I would like to go and just be a completely new person."

I drink my beer and watch the game like I'm an alien watching humans for the very first time. Mark's arms look too long for his torso, and Darlene's ears stick out at odd angles. All three pool players are these strange hairless creatures leaning over a green table and hitting balls with sticks. The longer I look, the stranger they seem. Lincoln is wearing a black T-shirt with a dizzy geometric pattern on the front, and Darlene keeps rolling the pool cue between her hands and blowing on the tip. Soon I can't even understand what they're saying or if it's English or how humans communicate.

Eventually I get tired of the game and find myself wandering upstairs for a snack and to possibly discover what other humans do in social situations.

I end up sitting alone in the front room with a two-foot-tall Jesus staring at me. He's spread out on a cross, almost naked like some S & M thing. There's blood and sweat all over his body, and one of his eyes is squinting.

That, or he's winking at me.

"Hey," he says. "What are you doing up here all by yourself?"

"I'm just hanging out," I tell him. "Taking a party break."

"Hanging out," he says. "Tell me about it."

I roll my eyes.

"Your friends are all moving away soon," Jesus says. "Don't you want to spend time with them?"

"I don't know what I want," I say. "Just leave me alone, okay?"

Jesus goes back to being crucified, and I pick a rose petal out of a bowl of potpourri on the coffee table. I eat it to see what it tastes like. Not very good.

"Did you just eat a piece of that flower shit?"

Melissa's brother Robert is in the doorway staring at me. He's got wide cheeks, and his eyes are too small for his face. Once Melissa and I walked in on him masturbating to a cooking show.

"Maybe I did," I say. "What's up?"

"I'm just … I'm looking for Neil. Have you seen him?"

"Sorry, not for a while," I say, but I feel like I should say something else, too. Jesus gives me the stink-eye from over Robert's shoulder, and the bass from the music downstairs vibrates through my feet.

"Cool," Robert says, and he turns and walks away before I have time to open my mouth.

A few weeks ago, I was at another party a lot like this one, and I was waiting for Robert to come with the whiskey I'd given him money to buy for me. It was late, and I was tired from work, and I drank water while I watched everyone getting drunk around me. I was in the kitchen when Mark asked why I wasn't drinking. I told him about the whiskey, and how Robert was already an hour later than he said he would be.

"I guess I shouldn't be surprised," I said. "Considering all the concussions he's had and how much weed he smokes, he can't have too many brain cells left."

Mark raised one eyebrow and coughed a fake cough, and I turned to see Robert in the doorway, looking out of breath and sweaty with my whiskey in his hands. He broke his nose playing hockey when he was younger, and it's always looked out of place on his face.

Robert looked over at me, then down at the bottle like it was an extra limb he was preparing to rip away.

"Here's your whiskey." He set it on the kitchen table and held onto the neck of the bottle while the party seemed to go on in an alternate reality around us.

I opened my mouth but no words came out, and as he was walking away all I could say was, "Thanks," so quiet I'm not even sure if he heard …

Robert has walked away again now, and it's just me and my empty beer bottle and this bowl of potpourri that will probably poison me if I eat any more.

In the kitchen ten minutes later, there is a pack of guys blocking the way to the sink. Robert's there, and he's found Neil. There's also Mark and Lincoln, who's high and laughing at everything everyone is saying, and this other guy with long hair and some kind of tattoo. I think I may know him from somewhere, but I'm just here to fill my empty beer bottle with water.

I slide beside the boys at the sink and keep my head down.

"What do you mean it was teeth?" Neil is saying.

"She had a bunch of gold-filled teeth in this little cardboard box."

My head turns at warp speed, so fast it almost falls off my neck. The guy sees me, and I see him like we're standing slightly above everyone else.

He stops talking. Water pours down the side of my bottle and over my hand. Everyone is looking at me, and I don't remember if I have clothes on.

"Tyler, tell Emily about this fucked girl," Mark says. "Was she on drugs or something? You must be coked out to try and pawn a box of teeth."

I wonder if I can fit my whole fist in my mouth.

"I don't think she was on anything. It wasn't that fucked," the pawnshop guy says.

"Didn't you say she started strangling herself at one point?" Neil asks.

"There was probably a lot of gold in those teeth. Maybe she just needed the money."

"Needed the drug money."

"Did you check? Was it just gums in her mouth? Was she trying to sell her own teeth?"

Maybe I can fit both my fists and my feet in my mouth.

"She sounds pretty weird," I say.

And the pawnshop guy glances over at me again and bites his thumbnail.

"There's been weirder," he says. "My uncle's told me stories."

"Like what?"

I step backward out of the room.

In grade-nine art class, our teacher told us about her favorite painting. It was a crowd, and there was a little girl's head in the mess of all the people that the painter hadn't attached to a body. The painter would never say if he'd done it on purpose or if it was a mistake. The girl's face in the painting looks exactly like my face does now. I'm having an out-of-body experience, but all I can see is my head floating through the air.

I've made it outside somehow. I'm sitting on the steps of the back deck staring into my beer bottle. I've filled it with the ocean, and now I need to build a ship small enough to fit into the bottle but big enough to hold me.

Melissa and Dan come out from the side of the house, but they don't seem to notice me sitting alone in this boat in this bottle. Melissa swerves across the lawn and slips on the dew.

"You are so fucking drunk," Dan says. He comes down beside her, and they lie on their backs to look at the stars.

I lie on my back, too, and the deck's wood slats press into me. With the sound barrier around Neil's neighborhood, you can't hear the highway from here. The silence is a mouth without any teeth, and I try to remember that there are people in North America, South America, Africa and Asia and all over the world being people and doing things that have absolutely no connection to me.

But the stars are too loud tonight. The mosquitoes are the stars, and they're eating me.

"There you are." I hear behind me. "I'm Tyler."

It's the guy from the pawnshop. He sits beside me as if I asked him to, and I have to sit up.

"Emily."

He sticks out his hand and I shake it. Here is my limb. I want you to hold my limb, and I will hold yours, and we will shake our limbs together.

I slap at a mosquito, and it leaves a blood mark on my arm.

"Listen," says the pawnshop guy, Tyler. "I didn't mean for that story to be cruel. It was just something I'd never seen. I'm sorry those guys took it like that. That's not what I meant."

We're both looking down at our feet. Tyler's got shorts on, and there's a bruise on his shin. It's a flower growing under his pale skin.

"It's cool, don't worry about it."

"No, it's not."

"Honestly, I've stopped caring if people laugh at me."

"Well, they shouldn't."

"I ate some potpourri while I was in the front room."

"What? Why?"

"Just a rose petal. I wanted to see what it tasted like."

"And?"

"Not very good. Don't try it."

He's bumped up right beside me, and the heat from his bare arm transfers into my bare arm like a subliminal message.

"So," I say. "How are you related to those people in there?"

"I met Neil at a show a few weeks ago. I moved here from Toronto last month."

"Cool. Why?"

He uses his thumb to crack each of the knuckles on his right hand. His fingers are made of wood, and he's breaking them all in half. He glances over at me, and in the light leaking onto the lawn from the kitchen window, his brown eyes are so dark they've absorbed their pupils.

"My mom lost her job," he finally says. "So we had to move in with my aunt and uncle. I'm just trying to save enough money to move back."

"Is it really so horrible here?"

"Last week two guys in a car with only three wheels drove by me. They'd propped the fourth corner of the car on this wagon thing, and one of them was sitting in the trunk holding the wagon in place."

"That's amazing."

"Yeah, but seriously."

"No, that's quality entertainment. You are not going to find that in Toronto."

Tyler nods and sighs. He's got the sigh of a fifty-year-old man.

I watch a mosquito land on his leg and I kill it for him, then pour some of my water onto his knee to wipe the little dead body away.

"Thanks," he says. He's got a long mouth and a scar like half a moon beside his eye. I can't remember if it's waxing or waning.

"There are other things, too," he says. "My sister's in Toronto, all my friends."

"We're your friends now."

"Fine, but if Cavanaugh's so great, how come every person I talk to can't wait to get out of here?"

"Because they don't know anything. There's a highway cutting through the whole town, and they think if they follow it they'll find somewhere better. Nothing's better, though. You can be unhappy here or you can be unhappy somewhere else. Being happy is more about how you see things."

"And you? You're smarter than that, and you'll stay here forever?"

"I'm not sure yet. I'm not as smart as I look."

I finish the last sip of my water and look into the bottle. A drip falls into my eye, and when I blink it out, it feels like a tear.

And then the shadows that are Melissa and Dan in the corner of the backyard come closer and turn into solid forms like ghosts turning back into humans.

"Hi, Em," Melissa says.

"Melissa, Dan. Tyler. Tyler. Melissa, Dan." I use my empty beer bottle to point.

"Hi, hi, hi," they all say, and Tyler leans back. He puts his arm behind me to support himself and leans over just enough so that we're touching.

But then Mark and Lincoln come out of the house and shout, "Let's go swimming!"

And more and more people pour into the backyard.

Suddenly our clothes are in a pile on Neil's deck, and we're all running in our underwear to Mark's pool down the street. Tyler is in front of me, and his back has been sculpted out of warm clay.

We sneak past Mark's house where his parents are sleeping, then take off sprinting again, down the hill to the pool protected from the outside world by a wall of evergreens.

My bra makes my boobs look lumpy, and I've got a hole in my underwear, so I cannonball in right away, and everyone else follows. We jump in over and over like we're trying to crack holes in the earth.

Melissa and Darlene float on pool noodles near the shallow end, and Dan cannonballs almost on top of them. Everyone comes up coughing, and even though it's dangerous to swim drunk in the dark like this, nothing bad can happen tonight. The whole world is breaking open just for us, and we are jumping into it again and again.

Tyler and Lincoln are at the diving board trying to do back flips into the water. They keep landing on their stomachs with loud smacks that echo above the trees, but they're laughing and laughing because no one can feel pain anymore, and all of us will live forever.

"I want to try," I call, and they clear a spot in the pool for me to spin myself backward into.

The diving board is rough on my feet, and my boobs still look weird, but it doesn't matter anymore because I'm invincible and about to perform a superhuman feat.

The board flexes, and all the stars in the sky are really inside of me. I'm in the air, and I'm higher than the tops of the trees. There's cool water underneath me, and I'm flying. I'm actually flying ...

Only I don't know what to do next. The water is coming fast, and I don't remember how to move my limbs anymore.

I land in a pencil dive, the exact same position I went up in.

When I resurface, Lincoln and Tyler are laughing so hard they're almost crying.

"Did I do it?" I ask, but they can barely speak. They're laughing and I'm laughing, and the night is an envelope we've been sealed inside of.

I climb back to the deck, and Tyler shows me how to flick my head back to do a flip.

"It should be one smooth motion all the way down," he says, and he runs his hand along my spine. Our faces are close together, and he keeps his hand on the small of my back as we watch Lincoln launch himself and land face first in the pool.

"I think I have chlorine in my brain," he calls. He swims to the side and reaches for my hand to help him out. I know he's going to pull me in, but I let him do it anyway and land on top of him.

Lincoln swims away and I race after him from one side of the pool to the other and back again, with this warm feeling on the small of my back.

We swim and we swim until we think we're maybe fish and maybe we were never born, and when we're not sure if we have limbs anymore we stop and lie on our backs with the night swirling around us.

Darlene lends me her pool noodle, and soon it's just me and Lincoln and Tyler and Melissa staring at a sky that looks like a painting. Melissa floats toward the deep end, but Lincoln tugs at her foot and pulls her close again.

"It's like the whole world is floating on something," Lincoln says into the darkness. "We are floating in a swimming pool built on a tectonic plate that's floating on lava, and there's air floating on top of us, and everything is floating through space. What do you think about that?"

"I think that you're probably high," I tell him.

"And hungry," he says.

"Me, too," says Tyler.

But none of us moves for a few more minutes. Tyler floats beside me, and his hand brushes against mine, but I'm not sure if it's by accident.

"Okay, okay, okay," says Lincoln after what seems like forever. "I'm getting really cold. We should probably go in."

We swim to the side and turn to see Melissa still on her back in the middle of the pool.

"You guys go," she says. "I'm just going to sleep here tonight." She waves her hand through the air like she's swatting away flies.

I grab her pool noodle and start pulling her toward the edge while Lincoln and Tyler stand on the deck and try not to shiver.

"Just leave me here," she says. "I'll be fine."

A breeze blows over us, and Lincoln and Tyler look longingly up the hill to their dry clothes and the party going on without them.

"It's okay," I tell them. "I'll get her out."

And they disappear through the trees.

I splash Melissa, but she lies still with the water running over her face.

"Are they gone?" she asks. Her voice is like a piece of driftwood bobbing across the water.

"Yeah, let's go." I splash her again, but it's like she's floating somewhere far away. The only sound is the water against the edges of the pool and the low rumble of music, like the party is a secret song we'll only know the words to when we get back to it.

"Come on," I say. I drag her to the side and take her pool noodle away.

She stands in the shallow end, and her eyes swirl from the tops of the trees to her wet bra to me waiting by the ladder, like she's trying to figure out what she's doing here.

"It's just us now," she finally says. "I don't want you to leave."

"I'm not the one who's leaving."

I have to help her out of the pool, and she's so drunk it takes seven hours to climb the hill to Mark's house. By the time we get back to the party the sun will have risen, and there will be nothing left of the night but a few beer cans on the lawn and someone barfing in the bathroom.

Melissa stops at the top of the hill near Mark's back door and squints toward the trees around the pool like she can't find her way.

"Come on," I say, taking her hand. It's the one that was cut up by the overpass, and the scabs have softened in the water.

"Just wait for a second," she says.

"No, let's go." I pull her arm, and she trips and grabs onto me to break her fall. Her fingers dig into my shoulders as I try to push her upright.

"Come here for a second," she says with her eyes still spinning and her body a deadweight on my chest. "I need to ... I need to tell you ..."

And then she kisses me on the mouth. It tastes like tequila and old beer.

"You are so fucking drunk." I try to shove her off, but she's surprisingly strong. She goes to kiss me again, and her nails cut into my skin.

"God, just get off me," I tell her, trying to twist from her grip.

"It's not that. I'm not drunk. I just didn't know how ..." Her legs have given out beneath her, but she's still hanging on, dragging me into some sort of hole. "Don't tell anyone, promise? I just don't want ..."

And then a man clears his throat behind us, and we turn to see Mark's dad in the back doorway. He's in his housecoat and slippers with knives for eyes.

"Girls," he says. "I think it's time you head back to the party."

Melissa and I are insects pinned in a display case. The only things we can move are our heads. We look down at our wet underwear, then back at Mark's dad.

"Now," he says.

"Yes, sir," says Melissa, struggling to get up. Her eyes are broken dinner plates, and there's blood in a wet snake down my shoulder where her nails dug in.

Melissa trips in Neil's driveway, and her knee is bleeding, and the house is bleeding sound from the music in the basement. Lincoln, Dan and Neil come out the front door and I head toward them, leaving Melissa to pick herself up.

"We thought you'd drowned," Lincoln says.

"We're alive," I tell them. "This drunk-ass tried to make out with me, though."

Melissa freezes in the middle of the driveway where she's examining the cut on her knee.

"Did you?" Dan's voice is deep and splits the night.

Melissa looks up at us with two fingers covered in blood from where she was poking her cut. There's a dark lip of mascara under each of her eyes like she's been punched in the face.

"God, of course not," she finally says.

"Did you?" Dan asks again.

Melissa spits and wipes her bloody fingers on her stomach, a streak of red across her skin.

"What is this, Dan? Some fucking interrogation?"

Dan tries to grab her shoulder as she brushes past us into the house, but she shakes him off. She slams the door behind her, and Dan follows.

Neil, Lincoln and I are left in the driveway staring at each other.

"And the award for couple most likely to murder-suicide goes to …" says Neil, and Lincoln and I stare at him.

"Oh, come on," he says. "They fight more than my parents do. Melissa probably only tried to make out with you so they'd have something else to argue about. They get off on it."

Lincoln looks between the two of us and heads back into the house just as Melissa storms out the front door. She has her shoes in her hands and her tank top is inside out. Dan chases barefoot after her, and we watch them make their way down the street, Melissa stomping at top speed and Dan jogging behind her.

By the time I get back inside, the party is starting to dissolve, and I feel like I've missed the whole thing.

I put on my clothes on the back deck and wander through the house picking up dirty cups and trying not to look like I'm looking for Tyler. He must have gone home, though, and now I'll never see him again. Of course it doesn't matter to Melissa that her fucked-up party-girl act wrecked my one chance with the only hot guy left in town. I'm just a sub-sub-sub-plot used to add tension and then abandon on the Melissa Desmond Television Drama Special. I hate to say it, but a part of me is happy that in twelve days she'll be moving to the very edge of the continent.

I take the cups to the kitchen and wait in the front hall for Lincoln. He's sobered up and is going to drive me home. The white fingerprints Melissa left on my shoulder are starting to go dark, and there are three red lines like cat claw marks down my arm.

"Emily."

I jump at Tyler's voice. He's pulled his long hair into a ponytail, but he's still not wearing a shirt.

"I thought you'd left," he says.

"I'm about to."

"Well, listen …" He cracks the knuckles on his left hand and pulls out his phone. "Did you want to maybe hang out sometime?"

The hallway is too small and there's a picture of Jesus holding a baby goat staring at us, but somehow I manage to move my lips and make sound come out of my mouth.

"Yeah," I tell him. "That would be great. I … I work tomorrow, but maybe the next day, Tuesday."

Tyler nods and I put my number in his phone. And then Lincoln is there and Tyler is gone, and the streetlights flash over our faces. We drive in silence out of Neil and Mark's neighborhood, over the overpass to our part of town.

"I guess that was the last one," Lincoln says. "The last party ever."

He pulls into my neighborhood and we watch the houses flash by like those flip animations you draw in elementary school — a man running or a baby carriage rolling down a hill, a slightly different picture at the edge of every page.

"There will be more," I say. "There are always parties."

"Not like that with everyone there. Neil's parents are coming home tomorrow, and people are going to school and stuff. I doubt everyone will come back, at least not at the same time."

He parks in front of my driveway and we stare at my house. I never noticed how small it is until right now. Most of the furniture was already there when we moved in, and the old owner's smells became ours. Maybe later another person will live here, and the house will forget we ever belonged to it.

"It was fun, though," Lincoln says. "For the last party ever, I'm glad that was it."

I don't know what to tell him, so I reach my hand up and touch his cheek. Everything seems so much smaller all of a sudden, and I feel amazingly old.

His cheek is warm and my hand is warm and he tells me, "Now get home safe." And I walk the thirty steps from his truck to my house.

5

I wake up with minnows in my stomach and a headache made of nails. The alarm on my phone is a high-pitched whistle and I let the sound go through me. It turns my bones to iron and then to rust, and all of my joints have fused together.

My room is covered in a layer of clothes two feet deep. Getting out of bed, I trip over a pair of jeans and the box holding my grandma's old teeth. All I want to do is crawl back under my blankets and wait for the world to sort itself out, but I've got to go to work and make one hundred million sandwiches for someone's funeral or baby shower or something, and Melissa will be there, too.

The marks she left on my arm have turned to purple fingerprints with the cuts slashing them out, and I already feel my patience with her dropping. Her dad's kind of an asshole, and since Robert stopped playing hockey, her mom's treated her like the family's last hope to have a successful child, but I don't know if I can spend another day locked in Pamela's basement watching her I'm-so-misunderstood-and-angry act. She used to put it on for other kids at school so they wouldn't bother us, but lately it's like she's forgotten it's a performance.

I make sure to put on a tank top so she'll see the cuts and bruises she gave me and feel a bit bad at least.

Only, when I get to work, Melissa isn't there. Pamela lets me in and I follow her orange perm into the basement to meet a girl a few years younger than me. She's already hard at work buttering bread for the cucumber sandwiches.

"Stephanie's my niece," Pamela says, taping her purple nails against the metal table. "She's going to be helping us out now that Lincoln and Melissa are moving away."

The girl nods and goes back to the bread. She's all eyes and elbows like a starving fawn.

"I've got errands, but you'll show Steph how to fill the order?"

"Of course," I tell Pamela. I've still got this hangover like my organs are made of damp blankets.

She disappears upstairs and I squint around the kitchen like it's a different place without Melissa and Lincoln here.

"I'm buttering the bread," Stephanie says. Her eyes take up most of her face.

"Okay," I tell her, and she looks away.

I'm too tired to speak so I turn on the radio in the corner and only open my mouth to tell Stephanie what to do.

"Have you worked here long?" she asks.

"Almost two years."

"Do you like it?"

"It's all right." And then we're quiet.

When Stephanie goes to the bathroom, I take two cucumber slices and press them to my eyes. I stand in the middle of the kitchen like that, listening to my breathing and my headache like a heartbeat in my forehead and feeling the basementness of this place.

Beyond these walls isn't a world of possibilities where every door is open and every road leads to an adventure. It's earthworms and gas lines and maybe the bones of someone's dead cat buried in a shoebox in a backyard.

When Stephanie comes back, she catches me with the cucumbers still on my eyes.

"Have you ever tried this?" I ask, peering at her from under one of the slices.

She shakes her head.

"They do it in all the movies," I say. "But I don't see what the point is."

She takes up two cucumbers, too, and we stand still in the kitchen, feeling these cool vegetables on our warm faces and waiting for the worms to eat our flesh away.

By the time I head back over the overpass, my hangover has lodged itself so deep in my body I'm afraid it might be permanent. It's too hot to make it home in one shot, so I stop at my grandma's for some water and to cool off.

"Why, it's Princess Emily," my grandma says. She's at the front door before I even get to the porch steps. "To what do I owe this pleasure?"

She sweeps me into the living room and disappears into the kitchen for drinks. Today the blinds and windows are open and a hot breeze blows through. The wind shifts the papers and doll hair and plant leaves.

"What day is it today?" my grandma asks. "Isn't it Monday? Didn't you have to work?"

I nod as she sets a glass of apple juice on a stack of envelopes in front of me.

"I was just walking home."

And I tell my grandma about the new girl, how she's so skinny that when we were carrying trays of sandwiches to the van I could see her spine through her shirt, and I was afraid her arms would snap in half.

"And what about Melissa and that boy? Don't they work there anymore?" My grandma's on the couch beside me, swirling the ice in her glass.

"They're leaving, Grandma," I say, and she nods along as I tell her about Melissa being nervous to take a plane by herself and how Lincoln has updated me with a "This Many Days Until Australia" countdown almost every day for the past three months.

"And what about you?" she asks.

"What about me?" The top envelope my glass was balanced on has a wet ring of condensation. I pick it up and fan it in front of my face.

"What are you going to do when everyone leaves?"

I press the damp envelope to my forehead, but it doesn't seem to clear my thoughts or cure my headache so I put it down and put my glass back on top.

"I guess it'll be different," I say. "It already is. All this summer Melissa's been practically ignoring me, and last night she was just so … she just acts like she's so messed up all the time. It's gotten really old."

My grandma stretches and watches out the window as a man pushes a lawnmower down the street like he's practicing to get a dog.

"In my experience," my grandma says, turning back to me.

"The ones who are so desperate for our attention are usually the ones who need our attention."

I shrug and she puts her warm hand on my warm forehead.

"You look sad," she says, and she moves her hand to my cheek and then under my chin. "I don't think you have a fever." As though that is a symptom of depression.

And then she puts her hand on my shoulder. Her grip is strong considering how thin she is.

"It's a good thing it's Christmas," she says. "No one can be sad at Christmas."

It's an old trick my grandma used to play. When we had to clean the house, we were nuns in an ancient church, and this was our penance. When I was upset, we were on vacation in a foreign country or it was some made-up holiday we immediately had to celebrate.

"Grandma, it's okay," I say. "I'm too old for this."

"Too old for what?" She steps over a broken rocking horse, an overturned flowerpot and Volume *E-He* of an encyclopedia to the bookshelf where she pulls out a VHS. A minute later a scratchy version of *The Muppets Christmas Carol* comes on the TV. It's the beginning of the tape, but the Ghost of Christmas Yet to Come has already arrived. My grandma stops for a minute to watch Kermit the Frog give a speech about Tiny Tim and how they'll never forget him.

When she turns to me there are tears in her eyes.

"That part gets me every time." She kicks a pair of pants and a part of an eavestrough out of the way to the window and looks up and down the street.

"It's so sad," she says with her forehead against the screen. "I understand not wanting to offend anyone, but I can't believe no one on the street decorated for the holidays this year. Not even the Hendersons."

"Grandma," I say. "You know it's not actually Christmas."

But she just blinks at me and tells me to get the tree from the basement.

"It should be in one of the boxes near the washing machine."

I take my time downstairs. It's cooler here, and with everything packed into boxes, the chaos seems more ordered than the mess upstairs. If it wasn't for my grandma's voice singing carols above me, I could curl up and sleep right on this bare concrete. When I woke up it would be thirteen years from now, and I'd find myself with a house and a husband and a baby on the way.

"Did you find it?" my grandma calls. "I think the ornaments are there, too."

The cardboard box is falling apart, with branches poking out like the tree inside is alive and has grown during the months it was packed away. I somehow manage to wrangle it upstairs, then crash to the couch with my hangover still on me like a bad dream I can't shake.

"We need gifts, too," my grandma tells me, sweating in her Christmas sweater. Two reindeer embroidered in chunky brown wool prance across her chest, and the sparkly snowflake sewn onto her shoulder dangles by its last few threads. She mutes the TV and presses Play on her Motown Christmas CD.

"*City sidewalks, busy sidewalks,*" she sings along. Termites gnaw through my skull while my grandma twirls around and around.

She's cleared a path between the tree and the fireplace where she's hanging up the stockings, and she waltzes with a sock in one hand and a paperclip in the other. She couldn't find the actual stockings, but she's improvising.

"I tried to check the weather," she says. "But all the papers are old. I'm afraid it won't be a white Christmas this year."

"Grandma," I say with my hands holding my headache in place. "That's because it's August." I peek between my fingers at where she's standing in the corner of the room with the Christmas-tree skirt in her hands. When she looks at me, she seems confused for a quarter of a second.

"Of course," she finally says. "We always celebrate Christmas in August. It's a Robinson family tradition." And she comes to where I'm lying and wraps the Christmas-tree skirt around my waist.

There's no resisting my grandma when she gets like this. I sigh and stand, and she twirls me in the skirt with my stomach lurching.

"Remember? You used to dance around in this skirt every year," she says. "You used to get so excited at Christmas. I've still got your letters to Santa somewhere. One year all you asked for was a harmonica and big feet."

"I remember that," I say, hanging a few ornaments on the tree. "I'd just started swimming lessons and the teacher told me you swim faster if you have big feet."

I get a chair for my grandma and hold her steady while she puts the star on the top of the tree. She always gets to do the star.

"Do you like Christmas morning or Christmas Eve better?" I ask.

"Christmas Eve. Definitely Christmas Eve."

"Okay," I tell her. I close the blinds and plug in the tree.

My grandma starts clapping, and I clap, too. This is the official tree-lighting ceremony.

I go to the kitchen for a plate of cookies and a glass of milk to set beside the fireplace, and when I get back to the living room, I look from the reindeer figurines to the wreath on the door to the tree with all the old ornaments on it, and suddenly something runs through me like warm molasses. It's dark and sad and sweet all at the same time, and I almost want to cry.

My grandma pats the seat beside her on the couch, and she turns up the volume on the TV. *Home Alone* is playing now, but it cuts into the last ten minutes of *It's a Wonderful Life*. The VHS is all the Christmas classics taped from television and layered over top of each other. *The Little Drummer Boy* and then *Rudolph the Red-Nosed Reindeer* in Claymation. I don't remember the videos until we get to them, and then each one seems oddly familiar, like at the beginning of fall when you pull out the cardboard box with all your warm clothes in it and find the sweater you forgot you owned.

We eat the cookies that were set out for Santa and microwave our apple juice to turn it into hot cider. My grandma falls asleep on the couch with *The Grinch Who Stole Christmas* flashing across her face.

When I finally leave, the sun is setting, and I blink at the flowers and the green grass and Cavanaugh's August streets like I've been teleported from a land that's only winter, and this is my first time feeling this wet summer heat on my skin.

6

The next day I'm woken by a knock on my bedroom door and Lincoln calling my name.

"Emily, wake up, I need you." His voice sounds like it's wrapped in cotton balls.

"Come in," I call. The room is full of this clear white light, and I'm not sure if it's morning or evening or if I'm still dreaming.

Lincoln sits at the end of my bed.

"How did you get in here?" I ask.

"Your dad let me in."

"My dad?" If my dad is home, it's still sometime before nine.

"Yeah, he's this super tall guy, middle-aged, kind of looks like an accountant."

"He's not an accountant," I say. "He's an environmental consultant." I close my eyes and throw my arm across my face waiting for this all to be a dream, but Lincoln pulls the blankets off and drags my arms until I'm sitting, still with my eyes closed. He pulls one of my eyelids open, but I pretend I'm still asleep.

I feel like I'm stuck at the bottom of something deep and warm, but it's no use trying to fight being pulled out. Lincoln wraps my arms around his shoulders and tries to fireman-carry me out of bed.

"Okay, okay," I say. "I give in. I'm awake."

He drops me back on the mattress and flops down beside me.

"What's happening?" I ask. "What do you need me for?"

"I have to buy shoes, like special hiking shoes but that I can wear every day."

I hit him in the face with my pillow, but I'm somehow coerced into his truck and driven half an hour down the highway to The Northern Lights Outdoor Supply Warehouse.

I keep one eye closed on the car ride there while Lincoln tells me about this video he watched that taught him how to pack a lot of clothes into a small bag.

"Even with that technique," he says, "I don't think I'll have room for more than one pair of shoes."

"Why?" I ask. "Where are you going?"

"Hello? Australia? Are you still asleep?"

"I think so," I say.

I don't think I'm fully awake until ten minutes after we get to the store, when I'm watching Lincoln limp up and down the aisle in a pair of cleats.

"What do you think about these?" he asks. "They're classier than running shoes, so I could wear them to a club and stuff, and then if I play soccer, I'll already have cleats."

I make him walk up and down in front of me a few more times.

"Look at how you're walking," I say.

"They aren't broken in yet, and besides, the soles are different from regular shoes. This is just how people walk in cleats." He walks toward his reflection in the mirror and pats down his backward hair.

"But do you really want to be known as that guy who walks funny and wears soccer cleats all the time?" I ask.

We look at the shoes and listen to the tap of hard cleats against hard tiles. It's still early, and there are only a few other people in the store. Most of them are families shopping for back-to-school sports equipment or else maybe stockpiling for the apocalypse.

I make Lincoln walk back and forth a few more times before he agrees to go with something a little more traditional.

"So, was Melissa like the most hung over at work yesterday?" Lincoln asks as we wander through the camping supplies.

"I don't know. She wasn't there."

"What do you mean?"

I pick up a filter guaranteed to remove 99.8 percent of all particles from water and read the label.

"There was a new girl there," I tell him. "Your replacement."

"Why? Where was Melissa? Is she okay?"

"I didn't ask."

Lincoln gives me a look like I'm suddenly speaking in tongues. I shrug and he pulls out his phone.

"What do you think would happen if you put juice in here?" I ask, swinging the filter in front of his face.

Lincoln blinks for a minute like he's trying to decide if I'm back to speaking English.

"Or blood," he finally says.

"Or chocolate milk."

"Eww."

"How is that grosser than blood?" I ask.

"I don't know. It just is." His phone buzzes and he turns back to it.

"She had a meeting at the bank," he says, as though I'm interested. "Her school was missing one of the forms for her scholarship, but it's sorted out now."

"Okay," I say. I lead the way to the display area at the back of the store. There's an AstroTurf lawn, a tent, a fire pit and two lawn chairs. I sit in one and Lincoln follows.

"Are you guys in a fight or something?" he asks. "Did she really try to make out with you?"

I shrug.

"Awesome," he says, pretending to warm his hands over the fake fire. "You two could be the new Becky and Elise."

Becky and Elise were these girls the year above us who started dating the summer after their graduation. It only lasted six weeks, but their names will be forever engraved on Cavanaugh's list of local celebrities.

"Yeah, right," I tell Lincoln. "Melissa was just being fucked. I'm just over the fact that she gets so wrapped up in her badass-rebel act that she forgets other people exist and have feelings."

I reach for a long metal marshmallow stick displayed beside some barbecue tools and use it to poke at the fire.

"I don't think it's that she doesn't care," Lincoln says, unconsciously patting down his uncontrollable hair. "Melissa is just ..."

"What?"

"She's a complicated woman, and that's why we love her."

I sigh and sit back in my chair with the marshmallow stick swaying in front of me like a divining rod.

"Next summer when you're back, we should go camping," I say. "But we won't take anything but a knife and see if we can survive."

"And if we don't survive?"

"Well, we would bring a phone for emergencies, and maybe alcohol, but it could be like that book *Hatchet*. Remember reading that in grade six?"

Lincoln nods, and a store employee in a red polo shirt walks by. He looks like he's going to say something to us about camping out in the display area, then changes his mind. Lincoln and I have made it so far into this artificial wilderness that they'll have to send in helicopters with rope ladders to get us out.

"If we're bringing alcohol, we might as well bring chips and stuff," Lincoln says. "We can hunt for our dinners, but you know how I like my snacks."

"We should bring sleeping bags, too, then, so that at least we won't be cold."

"I'm pretty sure this is just regular camping now," he tells me.

"I'm okay with that." I stretch in my chair and feel the fluorescent sun on my bare skin. There's a barbecue with fake hamburger patties set up to the right of our campground. I go over and flip them with a spatula as shiny as the moon.

"Only I don't think I'm going to be around next summer," Lincoln says.

"What do you mean?" I've got my back to him but I can see his tiny reflection in the spatula like he's far away already and I'm watching him on a television screen.

"Well, I'm going to be in Australia for a year, and afterward I was thinking of traveling around for a bit. Depending on how much money I can make, I want to take like four or five months and travel through Asia."

I flip the burgers again but they don't look nearly as appetizing up close as they did from my lawn chair.

"I thought I told you," he says.

"You did tell me. I guess I just didn't really think about it." I close the lid on the barbecue and turn the dials up high. "That sounds really fun."

A woman pushing a stroller walks by, and the baby inside is screaming. No one knows what the baby is saying and no one is doing anything to help it.

"I think I'm going to pack it in for the night," I tell Lincoln. "Make sure the fire's out when you come to bed." I crawl into the tent and lie on my back to stare at the orange roof and the tent poles spiderwebbing across it. Outside, the baby is still crying but its mother is pushing it farther away.

"Hey," Lincoln says, climbing into the tent beside me. "Are you upset?"

"No. I think I'm just tired." I feel a headache starting at the front of my scalp like tinfoil unraveling through my brain.

"Do you remember Neil's friend Tyler from the party on Sunday?" I ask.

"The guy with the long hair?"

I nod.

"He asked me out. We're going on a date tonight."

"A date?"

"I know. I don't know if I've ever been on a date."

"Hey, we went on a date." Lincoln unrolls one of the sleeping bags displayed in the corner of the tent and lies down like he really is going to sleep.

"I don't know if walking around the mall and then watching your dad play hockey really counts as a date," I tell him.

"Maybe not." He puts his hands behind his head and I unroll the other sleeping bag and lie down next to him.

"I guess I haven't been on a date either," he says. "But I've been thinking a lot about it." He rubs his nose and combs the bangs away from his eyes.

"Do you think there's something wrong with us?" he asks.

"What do you mean?"

"Well, everyone else goes on dates and meets people and connects with them and whatever, and we don't." His eyebrows are almost touching and he holds one hand in front of his face like he's trying to read his palm. "You'd think we would have gone on dates by now, right? I mean, it's not like we're ugly. People our age are having babies and stuff."

"It's just that Cavanaugh is tiny," I tell him. "Who would we meet? Is there really anyone around here you'd want to date?"

The fluorescent lights shine through the top of the tent and there are footsteps outside, but lying still like this, it all seems far away.

"I think I've got to be more emotionally vulnerable when I go to Australia," Lincoln says. "In my family everything is always fine and everyone is always happy."

"And that's a bad thing?" My eyes are closed now, but I hear him breathe out hard and shift beside me.

"Well, it's not really human, is it? I don't think you can really get to know someone and fall in love and whatever if you try to hide every time you're angry or sad."

And then there's a voice saying, "Excuse me, excuse me." And our tent is shaking. The store manager unzips the flap, and a face like a boiled turnip asks us to kindly exit the tent, pay for our purchases and leave the store.

Lincoln and I giggle halfway back to Cavanaugh, but eventually we go quiet. We stare out the windows at the fields and the forests and the scenery we've known our whole lives, and it feels like something in my chest is unwinding. I'll never be as young as I am right now, and there's no way to stop anything from happening.

"What are you going to do to be more emotionally vulnerable?" I ask Lincoln. My voice sounds strange cutting through the rumbling of the engine and the tired silence between us.

Lincoln keeps his eyes on the road and puts one of his chubby hands to his hair like he's searching in there for the answer.

"I think I'll just cry more," he says eventually. "I've always been taught to try and be happy and not to dwell on anything that upsets me, but I think sometimes it's okay to be sad. Instead of trying to, like, immediately make myself happy and forget about the sad thing, I'm going to try and feel it and not be ashamed about being sad and stuff."

"You think more girls will date you if you cry more?"

"Well, no one's dating me now, so it can only help."

7

Tyler is wearing a black T-shirt and jean shorts, and his long hair is combed out, a loose cape across his back.

"This is a nice car," I say, walking to where he's parked at the end of the driveway.

"Thanks, I'm just borrowing it."

The car smells like air after it's been through a hair dryer. We pull onto the road and drive toward the overpass with the hair-dryer air between us. Tyler's mouth is long and serious, and every time he turns the wheel the tree tattoo on his forearm shifts like it's blowing in the wind.

I watch the tattooed tree sway and the real trees outside the window and the cardboard air-freshener tree hanging from the rearview mirror, and my body suddenly feels like it's made of wood, too.

I should say something. People normally speak when they're in cars together, right?

Tyler takes a strand of his hair and puts it in his mouth.

"So, where are we going?" I ask.

"First, to get food."

"Oh, good. I'm starving."

And we're quiet again. We drive over the southern over-pass and I drag my tooth along my thumbnail. It exposes a white line in my red nail polish.

"Wherever we're going, I'm going to get a steak the size of my face," I say. "We should probably both get steaks." I chip off a bit more nail polish with my tooth and then sit on my hands so I don't accidentally eat them while I'm talking about eating things.

"Only if they have vegetarian steaks," says Tyler. "I've never been to this place before, but Neil told me it was good."

"You're not a vegetarian, are you?"

"I have been for almost three months."

"How? I love eating animals. If someone gave me a cat and was like, Emily, eat this cat. I would probably eat it."

We stop at a stop sign, and a man walking three dogs passes in front of us.

"What about a dog?" Tyler asks.

"Definitely."

"A human?"

"A baby or an adult?"

"A baby."

"Has it been named yet?"

"What does that matter?"

"It matters."

"Its name is Penelope."

"Then no. Maybe a Kathy or a Joanne."

"My mom is named Kathy."

"Well, if she was a baby, I would eat her."

The tires chew up the gravel parking lot as we pull in. Tyler parks the car and stares at the restaurant sign. It's written in yellow on a red background. All the words are the same size and the same font, making it look like the restaurant is called The Pearl Chinese Canadian Family Restaurant Dine-In Takeout Vegetarian Options Open Late.

There's an overworked air conditioner above the front door crying onto the sidewalk. It's after the dinner rush, and the only other people in the restaurant are a man and a woman at a table by the front window. Their faces are to their phones, and I imagine they're texting each other. They're about to be in a long-distance relationship and this is their trial run.

Tyler and I order our food to go and stare into a tank of sick coy fish. The woman from the table by the window comes to the cash to pay, then turns to me.

"Emily Robinson?" she asks, and I blink at her. She's spilled a drip of red sauce on the front of her white shirt.

"Yes?" I say.

"I thought that was you. I can't believe how grown up you are." Her face is doughy and her nostrils flare while she speaks.

I stare at her but I can't seem to connect any of her features with any kind of recognition.

"How old are you now?" she asks.

"Eighteen," I tell her, and the man behind the counter brings out our food in a brown paper bag.

"Well, I won't keep you from your dinner," the woman says. "But it was so nice to see you. You seem like you're doing really well."

As we leave, we hear her whisper to the man at her table, "That was Emily Robinson. She's the one whose mother …"

But we're out the door before we have to hear the rest. I'm tempted to rip my shirt off and go screaming through the parking lot just so she'll have a story for when she tells all her friends she ran into Emily Robinson at The Pearl Chinese Canadian Family Restaurant Dine-In Takeout Vegetarian Options Open Late, but then I remember Tyler's with me.

"Who was that?" he asks when we're back in the car.

"I have no idea." I've got the food in my lap, and I'm ripping the top of the paper bag into long strands so it will look like it has hair. "With my mother and all, I'm basically a celebrity."

"Why? What does your mom do?"

I stop mid-rip and look at him to see if he's pretending.

"What does my mom do?" I ask aloud. Tyler puts the car in reverse and we drive toward the highway. He doesn't look nervous or like he's waiting for a gruesome story.

He might be the first person I've met who doesn't somehow just know.

"Oh, she ... she just grew up in Cavanaugh, so a lot of people know her."

"Cool," says Tyler. "I guess everyone knows everyone around here."

"Yeah. It can be a little suffocating."

I let out a deep breath I didn't know I was holding and punch on the radio to change the subject.

We drive back over the southern overpass and around under it onto the highway with the windows down and the August air shooting in. Tyler drives fast — faster than I would ever drive. He nods his head along with the radio while I say it over in my head — *My mother grew up in Cavanaugh, and that's why a lot of people know me.*

I don't know where we're going, but the sky is clear, and driving out of town I feel clear, too. I'm a snake, and Cavanaugh's the skin I've been wearing for the past eighteen years. I'm fresh and raw and made of light. I turn around for a last look at the place where I grew up, the place that's kept me, and standing on the bridge looking over the northern overpass is a girl with thin brown hair and a wide nose. She's got a box of her grandmother's teeth in her hands, and she's wondering if she's going to spill them.

"I had this idea of where we could go," Tyler says, and he pulls off the highway at the first exit just past the sign that says *Cavanaugh, Thank You for Visiting Canada's Armpit*. The first five words are written in official-looking white letters, and the part about Canada's armpit is scrawled in black marker underneath.

We drive up a little hill and park in the parking lot of the bread factory. Tyler leads the way and I carry the food up a grassy incline to a view of the sun starting to drop and at least half the houses in town getting ready to turn their lights on.

"You've got to smell it," Tyler says, taking a seat on the grass. At first I can't smell anything beyond the paper bag holding our dinner. But slowly the smell of bread baking in the factory behind us rolls up the hill.

"Wow," I say. "This is fantastic." And we sit without talking for a few minutes, watching the night sew itself into the day.

Eventually, though, my stomach rumbles and I dig into the paper bag to pass Tyler his vegetarian combo.

"Do you like tofu?" he asks. He picks up a white cube with his chopsticks and we examine it.

"I don't know. I didn't the last time I had it, but I might now." I left my old skin back in Cavanaugh, and now I could be anyone. There's a chance I have a thick Spanish accent and an exotic birthmark over my right eye.

"Try some." Tyler passes me his takeout container, but the tofu is alive and keeps slipping from my chopsticks.

"Here." With his left hand he holds my chopsticks steady, and with his right he picks up a piece of tofu and balances it on my sticks. His hand is warm and his fingers have calluses on the tips.

"Not bad," I say, and when he smiles I see that half his teeth are slanted like they grew in in a hurry and didn't have time to settle in his gums properly.

"I'm officially the kind of girl who kind of likes tofu."

"And the kind of girl who goes to house parties and eats the potpourri," he says.

"I forgot I told you that."

From this far away Cavanaugh is a town in a model train set. With the smell of bread in the factory behind us and the stars just starting to come out it seems too precious to be a real town. Only robots and plastic train conductors could live there.

"What other kind of girl are you?" Tyler asks.

I stab one of my chicken balls and hold it up in the light from the setting sun. I eat tofu now. I can be anyone I want to be.

"I'm pretty good at math," I say. "And I like cooking and doing outdoor things, camping and fishing and stuff."

"I like camping, too." He tucks his hair behind his ears as though it will make him hear better, and when he looks at me he looks at me as though I'm a girl who's good at math and likes to cook and go camping and fishing. He shifts so that his knee is touching mine.

"So, what do you want to do?" he asks. He coils a long noodle around and around his chopsticks suspended in the air.

"What do you mean?"

"Like when you grow up." A warm wind blows by, and a leaf falls into my sweet-and-sour sauce.

"You don't think I'm a grownup?" I ask.

"Isn't your job making funeral sandwiches?"

"It's Pamela's Country Catering for All Occasions. It's just there are more funerals in Cavanaugh than any other occasion."

"Seriously, though, what about later?"

My dad and grandma and the teachers at my school always said it didn't matter what I did as long as I was happy. I read somewhere that kids whose parents die by suicide are three times more likely to do the same, but I guess I've always imagined myself doing something a little more than just not killing myself. I've always imagined being a cult leader in the middle of the desert or a pirate building a boat and smuggling dangerous animals into foreign countries. But boats make me seasick, and you have to be blond to be a cult leader.

"I used to want to be an actor maybe," I say. "You get to wear cool costumes and be a different person every show. But even then, you spend your whole life saying the same lines and recreating the same scenes like time is just repeating. I think after a while I would go crazy. Honestly, I think of all the jobs out there, and I don't know if I want to do any of them."

"Wow, that's bleak." The scar beside Tyler's eye wrinkles when he looks at me. His eyes are such a dark brown that if you poked one, your finger would come back covered in chocolate.

"Why, what do you want to do?"

"Right now I'm doing online classes to finish high school. Then I'm going to move back to Toronto, work for a bit there and study social work or something. Something where I can help people."

"Those are very serious plans," I say. "I'm a little jealous, actually."

Tyler shrugs. He moves his hand so that it brushes against my leg.

"It's easy to make plans," he says. "It's harder to actually go through with them." He sets his takeout container on the grass beside him and shifts closer.

"Maybe," I say. "If you know what you want." I slide my hand over so that my pinky is covering his. I can still smell the bread in the factory behind us, and a hint of Tyler's cologne. It doesn't smell like what a guy in high school would wear.

"Sometimes I think I want too much," he tells me. He flips his hand over and laces his fingers with mine. "I know I'm only twenty, but I don't want to wake up forty years from now and be, like, holy shit my life is almost over and I haven't done anything."

The sky is dark blue turning black, and before us is more than half of Cavanaugh, the baseball diamond, the hospital on the hill, Neil and Mark's neighborhood with the sound barrier around it and the highway, a yellow line of lights going beyond the town and cutting into the darkness. I know the highway leads to other towns and other cities and other people leading lives completely different from mine, but looking at the darkness now, it's hard to imagine anything beyond our town but a wide black field like an open mouth without any teeth.

"Maybe," I tell Tyler. "But Cavanaugh's all right. I wouldn't want to go somewhere or do something just to, you know, do something. I'd rather enjoy myself here and see what happens."

"What do you think is going to happen?"

Around us, lit up by the factory's fluorescent lights, the grass and the parking lot and the collection of trees to our right are all capped in gold, and when I turn to Tyler, his face is close to mine.

"Well, this is happening," I tell him.

And suddenly I'm not shy and I'm not awkward and I'm not something that happened fifteen years ago.

I'm Emily Robinson, and I kiss him and run my hands through his hair.

It feels different driving back into Cavanaugh. It feels like we were gone a lot longer than a few hours, like maybe I did peel some of my skin off and I am a different person than when we left. Tyler drives with one hand on the steering wheel and the other hand in mine, all along the conveyer belt carrying cars from high-rise offices in Toronto to three-story cottages farther north. We're the only car that takes the exit into Cavanaugh.

At the traffic light before my neighborhood, Tyler kisses my fingers and unweaves his hand from mine.

"It's funny," he says. "When you brought those teeth into the shop on Sunday, I kind of thought you were deranged." The stoplight's red glow makes his face shine when he looks at me. "And when I told Neil I was going out with you tonight, he made it seem like you were pretty weird."

"That liar," I say. "What did he say about me?"

"No, he didn't say anything mean. Ahh, I shouldn't have mentioned it. It's just that I'm happy we went out. And after you tried to pawn a box of teeth to me, I'm happy that you're not actually, like, a psychopath."

"I'm happy you're not a psychopath, either," I tell him.

When we get to my house, he leans over and kisses me, and it's hard to pull myself away.

"Let's watch another sunset soon," I say. "Wouldn't it be nice to spend your life watching sunsets and eating things?" And we kiss and we kiss, and I wave while he drives away.

When I get to my room, the box my grandma gave me is sitting on my dresser like it's been waiting for me, like I really am a psychopath who tried to pawn a box of old teeth. The parts of the teeth that aren't gold have gone yellow and brown, and each of them has an enormous root that used to be embedded in my grandma's gums.

"These were once a part of me," my grandma had said, as though it was a normal thing to give someone.

When I was seven and had just moved away from my grandma's, I was playing Underwater Space Explorers in the front room when I watched Mrs. Mack walk up my street and turn into my driveway. It was fall, and her otter-head poked out from a bright orange coat. She'd started volunteering in my class at the beginning of that school year, but I'd only spoken to her once when she took me into the hall to read a book about a rabbit that had a hole in its sock.

My dad let her in and got me to come say hello, which I did with the laundry basket I was using as a space helmet still on my head. Mrs. Mack's lips pursed together like they were trying to hide a mouth of tiny otter fangs, but my dad's laugh was like a dry cough behind me.

"Emily, can you take that game downstairs?" he asked.

I nodded, letting the basket slide around my head.

I stumbled around the basement for a bit with the alien invaders coming closer, but over my bloops and blips the voices from upstairs bounced off the bare walls and made their way down to me. I heard my name said enough times to forget my game and slowly creep up to listen in.

"I know the arrangement with her grandmother was only supposed to be temporary," Mrs. Mack was saying. The door was open the smallest crack, and I watched her at the kitchen table eating an oatmeal cookie with two hands. "If I'd known it would carry on for so long, I might have spoken to someone."

I couldn't see my dad from where I was crouching, but I heard him clear his throat and shift in his chair.

"I'm sure you've seen the disarray of the house," Mrs. Mack continued. "But I'm afraid it goes beyond that. Lillian has always been a bit off, and I don't know if she's been fully present since the ... well, the suicide."

My dad's large hand reached out from blank space and took a cookie from the plate he'd set in front of Mrs. Mack.

"I would just hate for her upbringing to cause any more damage to what's already happened," Mrs. Mack finished.

At the time I didn't really understand what she was saying. It was like someone was speaking in a dream. I knew what the words meant individually, but I couldn't string them all together.

My dad showed Mrs. Mack out soon after that, and their talk didn't seem to have any effect until a few weeks later when I told my dad I'd never been on a merry-go-round before. The next day he called me in sick to school and we drove the three hours south to the one-hundred-year-old carousel in St. Catharines. It was the end of November, and of course the carousel was already closed for the season, so we walked along the beach and threw rocks into the water. We had hamburgers for lunch and drove home later that day, almost without speaking.

And then it was back to normal again, only I still had Mrs. Mack's phrase embedded somewhere in the back of my brain. I found myself repeating it over and over, trying to get the words just right.

I would hate for any more damage from her upbringing to cause because of what happened.

I would hate for her upbringing to be for a damage to what already has happened.

I would hate for damage to be upbrought for her to hat what happened.

I said the words until they made even less sense than before, until eventually they had no meaning at all, and I tried to stop thinking about them altogether ...

I close the lid on the box my grandma gave me so I don't have to look at these teeth anymore, and then, as though my body is acting on its own, I watch myself walk down the stairs and into the garage. My fingers are on hinges slowly opening, and the box drops into the garbage can where it should have gone on Saturday when my grandma gave me these teeth in the first place.

I change into my pajamas and brush my teeth and go to bed.

I dream I'm taking Tyler to explore a cave at the bottom of the ocean. I leave him down there and swim through miles and miles of cool dark water by myself. I don't remember Tyler is even with me until I'm back on shore, walking along a sandy beach in another country far away.

8

It isn't until I get to work the next day that I remember Melissa will be there. She and Stephanie are in the basement already, and when I come downstairs they both turn to me but neither of them speaks. Melissa has eyeliner smudged under her left eye, and she looks like she hasn't slept or showered in days.

"Hey," I say.

"Hi," says Stephanie, and Melissa looks away.

They turn back to the tap where Stephanie is washing her hands. She works the lather from her wrists to her elbows and down under each of her nails. She turns her hands over and over in the steaming water, examining to make sure every part of every thing she's ever touched has been cleaned away.

She turns off the tap, and for a second the basement is so quiet it's like time stopped with the water. Then Melissa looks at me, and I roll up my T-shirt sleeves to show the yellow fingerprints she bruised into my skin.

Melissa takes her turn in front of the tap and then me, but I still somehow feel like we'll never be clean again.

Melissa brushes past me into the back pantry and I follow, watching a strand of greasy hair fall from her ponytail.

"You look like shit," I say.

When she looks at me something about her eyes makes her seem three hundred years old. She turns away without even acknowledging I'm there and gets out the ingredients for the stuffed mushrooms.

I follow her back into the kitchen where Stephanie is humming the theme song to a kid's show — either the one about the mouse who solves crimes or the dog who always loses things. Melissa stands on one side of Stephanie and I stand on the other, and Stephanie goes quiet. She looks once between us, then goes back to slicing cheddar and arranging grapes on the cheese tray.

Melissa pulls the stems from the mushrooms and I cut up crab, and our silence is an elastic band about to break. Melissa is not the only one who can play tortured youth, pout and give the silent treatment like we're twelve.

I toss the crab into a bowl and imagine I'm regurgitating the mayonnaise I slop on top of it. It slides up my throat and pours out my mouth in a creamy white mess. I stir everything together with an enormous fork while I wait for Melissa to finish chopping up the mushroom stems.

Pamela is on the phone upstairs, and her high-pitched laugh filters down and fills the space around us. Aside from the refrigerator motor and our shallow breathing, the laugh is the only sound, and the day creeps forward like a snail across a freeway.

When Stephanie goes for crackers in the back pantry, Melissa looks over at me, then down at her hand where the cuts and bruises from where she punched the overpass are starting to heal. I wait for her to say something — about the party on Sunday night, about what she did to my arm, about the fight she and Dan must have had after they left, or even about the weather or what she ate for breakfast. Anything.

But she turns back to the baguette circles she's spreading with cream cheese, and Stephanie comes back in. We're not alone again until the end of the day when I stop her on the stairs.

"Are you just not going to talk to me?" I ask.

She freezes with her back to me and one foot still in the air.

"Are you upset because I told everyone you tried to make out with me, or is it something else?"

She slowly lowers her foot but stares straight ahead with one hand gripping the banister and the other running her fingers through her hair.

"I don't … I don't want to talk about Sunday with you."

"Really?" I ask. "You're that upset? People make out when they're drunk. No one cares." She's the one who hasn't given a shit about me all summer. She's the one who practically attacked me after the pool that night. If I hadn't stayed behind with her she might have drowned. And now she's mad at me?

"You're blowing this way out of proportion," I tell her. "Not everything has to be some huge personal offense against you."

She turns slowly to look down at me with one hand still on the banister.

"I'm moving away in nine days," she says, and her voice is made of wood. "I just want to start new and forget you and Dan and all this shit ever happened."

"Why are you turning this into some giant conflict?"

With her free hand she makes a fist and looks for a minute like she's going to punch the wall or the banister or me, but instead she watches her fingers go limp.

"I'm just going to leave, okay?" she says.

"For school?" I ask. "Forever?"

But she's already started up the stairs again. There's a rip on the side of her T-shirt, and the hair that fell out of her pony-tail sways across the back of her neck.

"You don't even want to try to talk it out?" I ask. "After eleven years of being friends I mean that little to you?"

When she gets to the top of the stairs, she turns again to look down at me still standing at the bottom, and her eyes look more like the eyes of a horse than the eyes of a girl, large and brown and sad.

"Just leave me alone, okay?"

And before I have a chance to say anything else she's gone, and I'm left alone in this basement staring after her.

At the start of junior high there was this group of girls. They were horrible to me.

Every time I walked near them, they'd whisper, "Suicide Baby," and every few days they'd slip a drawing into my locker. Pictures of babies in straitjackets shooting blood out their eyes, or babies taking bites out of dead farm animals. Real artistic stuff. I usually tried to pretend it didn't bother me, but one day, just after Halloween, they filled my locker with fake blood. I'd barely slept the night before, and I'd gotten a bad mark on the geography test we were handed back that morning, and then after lunch I opened my locker and there was all this fake blood. It was all over my books and notes and gym clothes, and I stood there for a minute watching it pool onto the floor. It made a swirl on the gray tile, and the spot grew like a lake coming to flood a town.

As the blood spread across the floor, I felt blood on me, too. There was dried blood under my fingernails and behind my ears that I'd never be able to wash away. Everyone walking by looked at the blood on the floor and seemed to know about the blood on my skin. They knew I was unclean, and I could hear them all thinking, *Suicide Baby.*

Those girls were the scum of the earth, but they were only saying what everyone had been thinking my whole life.

Melissa came out of the cafeteria and saw me and saw the blood just as I was leaving. We still had three periods left, but I walked out the front door and down to the street, and Melissa followed.

I was so mad I could taste metal. I knew Melissa was there, but I was blind to anything but the cracks in the sidewalk. It was my mother who had left me like that, and now it was all anyone ever thought of me.

By the time I got to the cemetery, I was shaking so badly it felt like each of my veins was fighting against the others. I followed the path I'd taken with my grandma every year for the past ten years and there it was — a stone and a name and a date and some grass underneath. I glared hard and stamped on the ground, but already I felt a little silly storming out of school and walking halfway across town for a gray rock.

"What are you going to do?" Melissa asked. Part of me had forgotten she was there, and part of me knew she would always be there.

"I don't know," I said. "I don't fucking know."

Melissa and I looked at each other. I'd sworn before, but not the capital-F F-word.

"Fuck," I said again, and I let the air out of my lungs. Melissa had braces back then, and when she smiled the metal shone in the light. It was a freak warm day for November, and the sun felt artificial on my bare arms. It was daytime but the moon was out. It was almost a full moon, white and out of place against a blue sky.

"Fuck, fuck, fuck, fuck, fuck," I said, shaking my head. Each time I said it I felt older, until I was sure I was as old as the earth.

Melissa didn't seem to know what to do other than smile at me and nod every time I said fuck. She reached into her mouth to pull out a piece of food that had gotten stuck in her braces. She looked at it, then flicked it onto the grass.

"Fuck," I said again.

"Fuck," Melissa said.

We stood for another minute. The cemetery is far enough from the highway that we could barely hear the traffic, and after growing up to the sound of cars all day every day, any place in Cavanaugh that you can't hear the highway some- how doesn't feel real.

Melissa put her hand in mine, and it felt so warm and so small. Someone sucked the blood out of me and replaced it with silence as Melissa led me through the graveyard. Not to- ward the exit. Just around and around on the concrete path. Even the trees didn't shift as I read name and date, name and date. This woman lived to ninety-eight, this guy was as old as my grandma, this guy was as old as my dad. Melissa didn't say anything and I didn't say anything. Sun shone through the last of the orange and yellow leaves and through my body, and I was a drop of water in the ocean.

The path wound around a bend, and up ahead there was a family gathered around a hole in the ground like they were about to lower something down. They all wore black, and their chins were heavy.

We stopped walking when we saw the box. It was less than four feet long. The mother and father stood at the front of the little group and held each other up because their knees weren't working right. From far away they all looked so sad and so perfect, like the little plastic people on the tops of wedding cakes.

We backed away from them slowly. I wasn't paying attention to where Melissa was leading me. She held my hand and that was all I could feel. Around and around the concrete path again, and when we stopped walking we were back near the entrance of the cemetery. In front of us was a grave, already dug with no one in it and no one around. We stood at the edge with our toes over like at the swimming pool.

"Should we?" Melissa was still holding my hand, and her question was so quiet I wasn't sure if she'd said it aloud or if she'd just thought it and it had gotten to me through air.

I nodded, and we lowered ourselves in. Melissa first, then me. I almost turned my ankle on the drop down. I landed with a heavy sound that reminded me my body was still there.

Melissa and I lay beside each other, her feet to my head. I felt her body against me but I didn't believe she was there. It was at the bottom of the world, and all I could see beyond the square edges of the grave was the white moon on blue sky. I'd been left down there years ago, all alone with no way out and buried too far into the earth for anyone to reach. Every time I blinked the hole got deeper until I couldn't see the moon anymore, and I was sure I'd be stuck down there forever.

When I felt the wetness on my face, I didn't know where it was coming from or why it was there. I lifted my hand to wipe it away, but my hands were covered in mud and I had to just let the tears come.

I cried until my body shook and my lungs made the sound of the wind, and when I was finally dry Melissa sat up and looked at me. Her eyes were soft and serious, and she rubbed a streak of dirt from my forehead.

"It's okay," she said. "I'm still here. We'll always be together."

We went to her house after that. She took my muddy clothes off in the bathroom and ran the shower until it was warm enough for me to step in.

Afterward she wrapped me in a towel and made me hot chocolate. We ate popcorn and watched movies in her living room until her mom came home and yelled at us for skipping school.

9

Thursday and Friday at work are the same. Melissa and I are two ships in a harbor passing close by but never touching, and Stephanie is a deer with headlight eyes between us.

"Have you started packing?" I ask Melissa on Thursday afternoon.

"Sort of." And then she goes back to cutting the crusts off tuna sandwiches like she's in some sort of trance.

Usually when Melissa is upset she breaks something or punches something and gets over it. This new kind of theatrics just seems excessive. I can't tell if she wants me to apologize or ask her what's wrong or make her a little baby bonnet and tuck her into bed. All I know is that she's making me want to slam her head into the industrial bag of flour in the back pantry over and over until she gets over herself.

I've got the weekend off, and I lie in bed on Saturday morning feeling a lightness in my chest like a little fist unclenching. Lincoln's having a going-away party tonight, but that's not until later, so in the afternoon I borrow my dad's car and drive over the overpass to hang out with Tyler.

"When we get to the botanical garden, let's adopt fake identities and be new people," I tell him while he locks his door. He's wearing ripped jeans and a gray T-shirt, and his hair is a messy bun on top of his head.

"Who do you want to be?" he asks.

"I'll be Begonia Appleton. I ride horses and host charity luncheons at the summer home."

"She sounds terrible," he says. "If you're going to be some bougie baby, then I'll be an anti-capitalist anarchist."

"Perfect."

When we get to the botanical garden, Blaze Reinhardt, Tyler's alter ego, wants to sneak in over the back fence. He thinks nature should be free for everyone. Because I'm a rich girl from a rich family, though, I pay the three-dollar entrance fee for both of us.

"I was just joking about that capitalism stuff," Tyler says once we're inside. "I can actually pay."

I stop at a bush covered in purple flowers and smell one. It smells like this soap my grandma had when I was little, but also faintly of something chemical.

"Really, dear Blaze. There's nothing to worry about. Daddy gives me a generous allowance, and it's nice to enjoy the finer things in life with a peasant like you."

His hand is cool and rough in mine as I lead him to the center of the garden. We stand for a minute watching stone cherubs spit water into a fountain. Above us the clouds are breaking up, and a weak sun shines down. The sun hits against the water and makes the fountain look like rippled glass, and I feel some sort of cloudiness inside myself breaking apart as well.

"I think fat naked baby angels are the highest form of art," I say. I reach my hand under a stream of water and feel the cool baby angel spit on my skin.

"After the revolution there will be no art," Blaze says.

"Not even fat naked baby angels?" I make my eyes as wide as I can, and Tyler almost cracks.

"Life before beauty," he says with his hand beneath mine in the stream. "No one should spend their time making anything beautiful until everyone has shelter and enough to eat." He looks at his hand, surprised. This cherub water baptized him. His mind has been cleaned, and he can have brand-new thoughts.

I nod, but I'm Begonia Appleton and my whole life is ponies and flowers and diamond necklaces.

"But what about natural beauty like these blue things?" I pull Tyler toward a flower bed full of some sort of daisy. "Mother had the gardener plant a whole row of these last summer, but our dog Chester ate them all."

"Do you really have a dog?" Tyler asks as we head toward the greenhouse at the back of the garden.

"Why, yes. He won best in show three years running at the ladies' auxiliary charity dog show."

The greenhouse is where they keep the cacti. It's hot and dry in here like we're in some futuristic mini-desert.

"We had a dog when I was really little," Tyler says. "It was my dad's from even before he met my mom." He reaches toward an angry-looking cactus but changes his mind and puts his hand back in mine.

"It's funny," he continues. "The only time I've ever seen my dad cry was when that dog died. He didn't even cry when my grandpa died."

There's a cactus like an octopus hanging from the ceiling with long tentacles growing toward us.

"Are your grandparents still alive?" Tyler asks.

I walk farther into the greenhouse where little cacti grow out of red dirt like plant life on Mars, and I tell him my grandfather is the First Duke of Kentington Station.

Tyler stands in front of me and grabs onto my shoulders.

"Stop," he says. "I want to know." And then he kisses me right in the middle of the greenhouse for all the plants to see.

"My dad's parents live in Alberta," I say when we break apart. "I don't see them very often. My other grandpa died when my mom was fifteen, but my grandma lives a few blocks over from me."

Almost unconsciously, Tyler goes toward the garbage can in the corner and picks up a coffee cup lid that's fallen on the floor. He puts it back in the bin and grins at me.

"And what's your grandma like?" he asks.

"What's she like?" I imagine what Tyler's face might look like if I told him my grandma and I used to play a game where I was a dog with rabies. I'd run around the house with toothpaste drooling out of my mouth, and she'd pretend to beat me away with a newspaper.

"Oh, you know. Just like a regular grandma. She's funny, I guess."

"And are you guys close?"

She half raised me and was my only family after my mother's suicide until my grandma tracked my dad down four years later.

"Pretty close," I say. "It's nice that she's just down the street."

"I know what you mean." Tyler leads me out of the greenhouse and back toward the fountain with the fat babies spitting water. "There's still no way I'd stay in Cavanaugh if I didn't have to, but it has been cool to live with my aunt and uncle and actually get to know them."

The sun is out full now, and as we pass under the fountain I dip my hand in a stream of angel spit and rub cold water on my forehead and the back of my neck.

"I never really thought about it before this summer," Tyler continues. "But your family is your only constant, really. It's kind of cool to hang out with people who remember you from before you remember existing, and to know that they've always got your back."

"I guess you're right," I say. "I've never really thought about it that way, either."

On the way home we stop at the fry truck in the parking lot behind the mall. We park in the shade at the edge of the lot and lean against the hood of the car with a jumbo-size box of fries between us.

"These aren't even that good," I tell Tyler. I pick out a long fry and fling it to the seagulls swarming toward us. "I just like the idea of having a place on wheels that you can move around whenever you need to."

Tyler nods, then dodges as a seagull swoops at our heads.

"This truck has been parked here my whole life," I continue. "My grandma used to take me every time we went to the mall, but I just know that one day Greasy Peter — or whatever his real name is — is going to drive away."

Tyler nods again and we look back at the man in the fry truck. He's about fifty, bald and lumpy with a layer of sweat shimmering across his skin. He stands with empty eyes looking out the order window toward the highway like he's planning his escape.

When I get home, I find my dad at the kitchen table looking back and forth between his computer and some sort of instruction manual. Papers and discarded packaging are scattered all around him as well as sheets and sheets of plastic pieces. They're waiting to be punched-out and assembled into some sort of annoyingly accurate model to go beside his exact replica of the *Hindenburg* and *Apollo 11*.

"Take a look at this," he says before I can disappear from the doorway. "It's a mini-Strandbeest." He finds the box on the floor and holds up a picture of a spiny white machine, sort of like a centipede made of drinking-straws with a windmill on its butt.

I give him a blank stare.

"Come watch the video," he says, typing. "Clem's coming over tonight to help me put it together."

I sit beside him at the table and we watch these ten-foot-tall machines scramble like insects across a beach in the Netherlands.

"They're completely self-sufficient," my dad says. "In the future the creator wants them to live on their own in herds by the sea."

The video finishes, and my dad goes back to the instruction manual. His forehead wrinkles, and there's a dry patch of skin on the side of his neck. I imagine him slowly morphing into an enormous plastic animal, walking back and forth across the beach with a stunned look on his face.

"Cool," I say, and I pat him on the top of his bald head.

I'm almost out the door when he calls me back and says, "I meant to ask you. I saw this in the garbage can and I wanted to make sure it didn't get tossed in there by accident." He shifts through the papers and plastic pieces to produce the square box holding my grandma's teeth.

"Oh, those."

He opens the box, and we stare down at the yellowed bones capped in gold.

"I bet you can guess where they came from," I say, and he starts to laugh.

"No one can say your grandmother's not unique." He passes the box to me and I put the lid back on.

"That doesn't mean I have to keep her old teeth." I flip the box over and there's a wet mark on the bottom from whatever was in the garbage can below it.

My dad shrugs and turns back to his toy.

"You know," I hear him say when I'm already halfway down the hall. "Gold is a heavy element. All the gold that was originally on the earth sank to the center while the earth cooled."

I stop and turn back.

"The gold we find on the surface now came from outer space." He's framed in the doorway like he's on a television set. His eyes are green like mine, but I got the rest of my features from my mother. "There was a meteor shower almost four billion years ago, and the gold on the earth's surface is literally from those shooting stars."

I look down at the box and imagine its contents coming down from space and billions of years later ending up in my grandma's mouth.

"Is this like when you told me my Barbie was made of ancient sea creatures?" I ask.

He shrugs. "Barbies are made of plastic, plastic comes from oil, oil comes from microscopic plants and animals living in the ocean millions of years ago."

I roll my eyes, but instead of heading to the garage to throw the teeth out again, I take them to my room and push them to the very back of my closet for a future version of myself to deal with.

10

In the evening I go to Lincoln's for his Farewell to Canada Formal Departure Feast.

There are eight of us in our fanciest clothes, and Lincoln and his mom have cooked a four-course meal. We sit with his parents at the dining-room table and drink wine and listen to classical music.

"So," I say to Neil, who's beside me. "I've been hanging out with your friend Tyler, and he told me you told him I was some kind of psychopath."

Neil is wearing a suit jacket with a T-shirt printed to look like a tuxedo shirt underneath. He pauses with his soup spoon halfway to his mouth and looks around, but everyone else is sunk in their own conversations.

"I ... ah ... I didn't mean it like that. He just asked what you were like, and I said you were kind of weird."

I pick up the dinner roll from his plate and take a bite of it, then put it back.

"It's okay," I say. "I am kind of weird."

Lincoln's dad makes a toast, and we all hit our glasses together.

Across the table, Lincoln's mom is talking with Mark about American politics, and we all look so old all of a sudden. Maybe it's just our fancy clothes, but we aren't really kids anymore. There's Melissa whose hair is back to brown after being dyed every color of the rainbow. There's Darlene who used to pretend to faint every gym class so she didn't have to run, and there's Mark who took a tuna fish and pretzel sandwich for lunch every day of elementary school.

And now we're all saying, *Please pass the butter. I really like these potatoes. What seasoning did you use?* Like we're real adult human beings.

I excuse myself, and after I go to the washroom I follow the hall to Lincoln's room. The party goes on behind me as I open the door and peek my head in.

There's an enormous travel backpack on the floor and a set of clothes on the desk, already picked out for the morning. It's Lincoln's favorite striped shirt, jeans and his green boxers with four-leaf clovers on them. They're the boxers he's worn for every test and every exam for the past two years.

"Who wants coffee and who wants tea?" Lincoln's mom asks downstairs.

I expected Lincoln's bags would be packed and his clothes would be picked out, but I didn't realize the walls would be so empty. He used to have a collage of pictures above his bed — the time we drove to the beach, camping, a few of him and Neil as the fattest kids I've ever seen.

All that's left now are scuff marks on the paint and a few pieces of sticky tack.

There are footsteps down the hall, and Lincoln finds me on his bed with his striped T-shirt in my hands.

"Everything's gone," I say.

He scans the room and squints down at me. There's gel in his hair, but it's still as hopeless as ever.

"Mum and Dad are turning my room into an office," he finally says.

"Oh."

"Yeah."

"So you really are leaving," I say.

He looks out the window and I look at the floor, and when we look at each other we look as though we're frozen in a picture of ourselves.

We don't remember how to move until his mom calls, "Linc, we're just about ready for cake down here."

Back at the party, it feels as though someone turned the volume down. The candles lit during the meal have sputtered out, and the overhead light makes everyone seem too young and too small. Lincoln comes around with flourless chocolate cake and ice cream, and his mom brings out the tea and coffee, but it's all done at half speed and half sound as though we all know we're dissolving, but if we move very gently we might be able to keep it from happening for a little while longer.

Of course it happens anyway. Melissa, who kept her head down and barely spoke all dinner, leaves first with Darlene. And then it's Mark and Neil, then Lincoln's friends from the debate team, and soon it's just me and Lincoln sitting at his dining-room table with all the dirty dishes between us.

"I guess I should go, too," I say to the tablecloth. There's a yellow spot near the edge of it where Neil spilled his soup.

"You don't have to. I'm not going to be able to sleep anyway, and it's such a long flight, it's probably better to be tired for the plane."

And so I stay. We take the dishes to the kitchen and watch TV in the basement. Nothing's on, but we watch anyway because we're not sure what to say to each other anymore. I keep looking at Lincoln and thinking, *Remember this moment and remember how he looks,* but it feels like I'm grabbing fistfuls of water out of a lake.

"I hung out with Melissa on Wednesday," Lincoln says over a talk show rerun where they're turning shy teens into beauty queens. "She seemed pretty messed up."

"She's always pretty messed up. It's kind of her thing."

"I don't know about that. Maybe there's a lot going on for her right now." He undoes his tie and sits cross-legged with an orange pillow on his lap.

There's a lot going on for everyone right now. I have no idea what I'm doing with my life. All my friends are leaving Cavanaugh, and pretty soon I'll be stuck here by myself.

I don't say anything.

"Did you hear she and Dan broke up?" Lincoln asks.

I look over at him with the TV light flashing across his face. I'm surprised I haven't heard, but then again Melissa isn't talking to me and everyone else has been too busy getting ready for the mass exodus to hang out.

"That's not really a surprise," I say, but even though Melissa and Dan fought all the time, a part of me imagined they'd still be together at eighty-five, a fucked-up version of high-school sweethearts.

"They've been on-again off-again since they got together," I continue. "I can't feel too bad for her." And I try not to picture the way Melissa brought her fork to her mouth to-night, chewing as though she couldn't taste and it wouldn't matter if she could.

I shrug and turn back to the television. If she's going to blame her breakup on me telling everyone she tried to make out with me, then maybe she shouldn't have gotten so drunk and done it in the first place.

"I just think you should talk to her," Lincoln tells me.

"Yeah, maybe." I take a pillow and put it on my lap, too, like I'm trying to build a wall between us. On TV there's an ad for a new flavor of chips. A group of dogs chases a clown down a hill and they all end up in a swimming pool.

"Remember when we went camping last summer," says Lincoln. "And you drank so much you threw up in your sleeping bag?"

"Don't remind me."

"Everyone wanted to make you sleep outside, but Melissa cleaned you up and let you share her blankets."

I nod, but I only vaguely remember this part.

"Melissa just has a hard time dealing with things some-times, but you two have got, like, true friendship. It seems stupid to let it go."

I nod like I care and then turn toward the television, but in the back of my mind the edge of a memory I've been trying not to think about curls up and pokes its way forward.

I slept over at Melissa's house one weekend last summer. Robert and her parents were out of town and it was just the two of us watching movies and drinking her dad's liquor cabinet.

"I can't control it sometimes," Melissa told me deep into the night. I'd spilled pizza sauce down the front of my shirt, and we were both in the shower with our clothes on.

"I just feel so trapped inside everything," she said. With the wet sweater sticking to her shoulders, she was a bird rescued from water just before drowning. She started shivering, and I turned the shower hotter.

"Look," she said. She took off her top and shifted so I could see the underside of her arm. With the steam and the water drops in my eyes it was hard to make out, but on the tender skin below her bicep were faint white lines and a few red cuts healing over.

You are a bird, I thought, *and you are about to fly away.*

"How long has this been happening?" I asked.

"Forever."

She moved away and leaned back against the wall of the tub with her scarred arm hanging out the side.

"It's so stupid," she said. "It doesn't even make sense."

That night we lay in bed with our wet clothes left in the washroom sink. Our bodies were on separate sides of the bed, and I reached over to touch Melissa's arm where the scars were.

"I don't think this is good," I said. "I think you should stop."

"How?"

The night was eating our skin. We were dissolving into it.

"I want to know how to help you," I said.

We woke up a few hours later. It was six o'clock with the beginning of the day creeping through the curtains. We were still drunk, but neither of us was tired.

We put on clothes and got the leftover pizza from the fridge. We sat under blankets on the porch eating while this gray early-morning rain fell on the empty road.

Even the highway seemed quiet.

"Listen," I said as a man and a dog walked by. "About your arm."

Melissa brought her knees into her chest and pulled the blanket tighter around her.

"I was being dramatic. It's not a thing. It's not a big deal."

"But I mean if you're — "

"I'm not." She looked at the house across the street. The driveway was cracked like the earth had tried to draw a map in it. "There's nothing wrong. I shouldn't have said anything."

It wasn't the kind of rain that makes a sound. It was silver confetti.

"Are you sure?"

"Yes, okay?" She stood and spat over the railing into the garden.

"Okay," I said.

She paced across the porch like she was looking for something. Another man and another dog walked by, or it could have been the same man and the same dog as before. Melissa jerked forward and tore the lid off the empty pizza box. She ripped it into a heart and handed it to me.

"Here," she said.

"Thanks."

I walked home in Melissa's sweatshirt and jeans with my wet clothes in a plastic bag. My dad was still asleep when I got in. It was just after seven. I went back to bed and when I woke up that afternoon it was almost like nothing had happened, only I was still wearing Melissa's sweater with my wet clothes in a bag ...

"Can we go get cookie dough?" Lincoln asks. We're watching an infomercial for a set of knives that will cut cans, but we've both seen it at least four times already. I'm still so full from dinner, but Lincoln nods at me and scratches a pimple on his face, and I think we both know that for the next twelve hours until his flight takes off, I'll do anything for him.

It's almost three, but Lincoln's mom is still awake washing dishes when we come upstairs and grab the keys to the truck.

"We're going for cookie dough," Lincoln says.

"At the grocery store?" his mom asks. "Can you pick me up some eggs?" Her hands are bright red from the hot water but she doesn't look tired. She looks like it's the morning and she woke up to make breakfast only she realized there aren't any eggs.

She gets us money from her purse and we drive through our sleeping town, the only vehicle on the street.

"This is so weird," says Lincoln. "I'm driving through these streets I've known my whole life, and I'm thinking I don't live here anymore. This isn't my home."

I look at the side of his face while he looks at the road. He got his right ear pierced in grade eleven, but the piercing got infected and he took it out after a week. There's still a mark on his earlobe where the hole was punched through. I'm not sure if I actually see it now in this dark truck on these dark streets or if I just think I see it because I've seen it so many times before.

"Why are you looking at me like that?" he asks.

"I'm just looking at your face so I remember what you look like."

"That's what the internet is for."

The twenty-four-hour grocery store in Cavanaugh opened a few weeks ago, and there are only three other cars in the parking lot. We park near the doors and see Melissa's brother Robert at the other end of the lot. He's wearing his green grocery-store vest and collecting the stray carts that rolled or were pushed toward the patch of dead grass near the fence that separates Cavanaugh from the highway. He pushes a cart forward across the asphalt but its twisting front wheel skids on a crack in the pavement, and the cart crashes onto its side. Robert runs and plants a kick against its metal cage. He runs back, then kicks the cart again. He kicks the cart, kicks the cart. Picks up the cart by its corner and launches it to crash against the asphalt. The sound of metal on pavement echoes over the empty lot, and from this far away Robert's face is a fist.

As far as I can tell, Lincoln and I are the only customers in the store. Lincoln leaves me to pick out eggs while he goes for cookie dough. He walks down the long empty aisle as though he's getting smaller instead of farther away.

I flip open the damp cartons of cold eggs, but they all seem wrong. The eggs aren't white but this beige-yellow color with little lines drawn on them. There's a crack down the shell of at least one egg in every carton like they've all been out of their nests for too long. They couldn't handle being alive anymore, so they cracked.

It feels like I'm seeing these eggs from a long way away. I have to stop and look around to remember where I am and what I'm doing here. When I look up, though, I realize I'm in a grocery store, holding cartons of broken eggs in the cold air of the fridges in my party dress at three in the morning. In front of me are empty aisle after empty aisle of brightly colored food boxes and freezers so new no one has had the time to take the window stickers off yet, and here are these weak beige eggs, a cracked egg in every carton, and I don't know why, but I've got this gritty salty taste in my mouth, and suddenly I want to cry.

"Emily, can I help with something?"

I'm still standing with a carton of cracked eggs in each hand when I turn and find Robert behind me.

"All the eggs have cracks in them," I say, and we both look down at the cartons of eggs like the cracks aren't just about the eggs but about life, the universe and something enormous and buried that's been troubling us and all humans for as long as humans have existed.

"Here," Robert finally says. He trades the two cracked eggs from one container with two good eggs from another and then smiles. When he smiles his face goes wider, like it's one face that's about to become two.

"Thank you," I say. And we look at each other until Lincoln emerges from the back of the store. He walks toward us, bigger and bigger until he's so big it would be impossible for him to ever disappear.

Lincoln and I don't know what to do now that we've got the cookie dough. We sit in his truck in the parking lot and we watch the cars on the highway through the chain-link fence.

Lincoln looks at me and I look at him, and then we look away.

"Remember the olives?" I say.

"That was the best."

Last fall we were cleaning out the cupboards at Pamela's and we found a gigantic jar of expired olives. It was pouring rain that day, and instead of throwing the olives out we poured the entire jar over the overpass onto the highway. We wanted everyone driving below to think that they lived in a world where on very special days it rained olives instead of water ...

Lincoln looks at me and I look away again.

"Well," he finally says.

"Well," I say. "I guess I should go home."

"I guess so."

As Lincoln drives back over the overpass to my neighborhood I keep expecting something to happen. There should be fireworks or a car crash that leaves us horrifically maimed to mark that this moment is happening and that all of this is real.

Lincoln is already turning down my street, though, and now we're looking at my house and I'm trying to think of a way to tell him he's the very best person I know, and I'll miss him, and he deserves all the good things in the world.

"Have a nice trip," I finally find myself saying.

"Thanks. I'll let you know when I get there and figure out what I'm supposed to be doing."

"Good," I say. "Don't forget about me."

We have an awkward hug across the armrests, and then I'm on my driveway and he's waving and watching me walk toward my house.

The night after Lincoln's Farewell to Canada Formal Departure Feast, my dad is in the basement watching some sort of special on the ocean, and I'm in my room reading a book about black holes that my grandma gave me. The documentary narrator's British accent mumbles up at me through the floorboards, and I keep reading the same sentence over and over.

The star will collapse under its own weight.
The star will collapse under its own weight.

Somehow it got dark outside without me noticing. The window is a black and glassy sheet.

The star will collapse under its own weight.

Eventually I drop the book and stand at the top of the stairs to look down at my dad in the basement. He's got a half-finished crossword in his lap and his face is lit up by pictures of the ocean. He turns from the television and waves at me standing above him.

"What are you watching?" I ask.

"It's called *Dangers of the Deep: Jellyfish of the Pacific Ocean.*"

I get a glass of water and join him on the couch.

"How was your day?" he asks.

"It was good. I just went for a walk and then to the mall. I didn't buy anything, though. Not even fries." An enormous tentacled creature swims across the screen with blue-green water all around and smaller fish in the distance.

"You're not going out tonight?" my dad asks.

"No, everyone's busy getting ready to move to school and stuff."

"Oh," he says. The divers on the screen come across a jelly-fish twice as big as they are.

"Have you given any more thought to coming to Montreal with me?" my dad asks, but I shake my head.

"Well, let me know." And he turns back to the television where three divers are surrounding the enormous jellyfish. One of them approaches it with some kind of measuring device.

"It's funny," my dad says. "Humans have been on earth for over two hundred thousand years, but after all that time, the oceans are so big and so deep that we've only managed to explore ten percent of them."

Tiny red jellyfish blink on the screen, and the camera cuts to a scientist staring at a tentacle through a microscope. Later the divers swim deeper into the ocean and the water around them turns from dark blue to almost black.

When the documentary is over, my dad goes upstairs to make us a snack but sticks his head down a few minutes later.

"I can't remember," he says. "Is it butter you don't like on your popcorn or is it margarine?"

"Neither," I tell him. "They make it too soggy. I just like salt."

He bends like a paperclip so he can see me down the stairs.

"Really?"

"Yes. Always."

I pull my phone from my pocket while I wait for him, but I haven't got a single text. It's just me and my dad and the darkness outside the window and an ocean so deep no one knows what's at the bottom.

11

It's Monday. I've only been away from work for two days, but the basement at Pamela's Country Catering seems different now that Lincoln has left. The walls are closer together and the ceiling sags down like he was the one who was holding it up.

There's a note on the long metal table with a list of what I'm supposed to do for the day. Pamela is visiting her mother, and Stephanie has a stomachache. It's Melissa's last day at work, but she's going to be late.

The note finishes with, *Think of this as a test run, Emily. There could be a real future for you here at Pamela's Country Catering.* She's drawn a winky face and signed it ~ *P.*

I stare at the note and imagine myself spending the rest of my life in this shrinking basement, boiling eggs and making pastries until my head hits the ceiling and my bones fold up with the walls.

I slide the note across the table so I don't have to look at it, then turn to my cooking-show studio audience.

"Today we've got some simple rabbit-brain tea sandwiches on order," I say to the camera. "You want to boil the skulls for at least ten minutes to make sure the brains are cooked through. And while those are on the stove, I'll start on the barracuda heart puree and take questions from the audience."

I open five cans of tuna and drain them into the sink.

"Hi, everyone," says an imaginary woman with imaginary horn-rimmed glasses into the imaginary microphone. "First, I want to say I love the show."

"Thanks."

"But who are you, and where is Head Chef Lincoln?"

"Excellent question," I tell her while flattening the tuna with an enormous fork. "Unfortunately, Lincoln is no longer available, and I will be taking over his position as head chef."

The woman drops the microphone and walks off.

"Where did he go?" asks the next member of the audience. "This show is nothing without Lincoln."

"Don't worry," I say. "I'm here to provide you with the same quality programming we've always had." But already other members of the audience are packing their things.

"Look," I say. "This bread is made of elephant feet." But in less than a minute, the entire studio audience has walked off the set and I'm alone making tuna-salad sandwiches in Pamela's basement morgue.

When Melissa comes in, she reads Pamela's note without speaking and gets to work with her head down.

I watch her cutting vegetables out of the corner of my eye and think about her arm in the shower last year with the cuts all over it.

She squeezes ranch dip into a serving bowl, but the plastic

bottle is almost empty. It sucks in air and the dip splatters across the table.

"Here," I say, handing her a cloth.

"Thanks." She wipes up the spill, then tosses the cloth back into the sink.

"Good throw," I tell her.

"I've been working out."

"Me, too," I say. "But only my thighs. I do three hundred squats and one hundred glutes a day."

"Glutes are muscles," she tells me, going back to the dip.

"Then what am I thinking of?"

She doesn't respond.

"Burpees," I say, turning to drain the eggs boiling on the stove. "That thing where you do a pushup and then you jump."

I leave the eggs to cool, and when I look back at Melissa she's arranging broccoli trees on the veggie platter. Her bottom lip is in her mouth, and a strand of curly hair falls in front of her face.

I cut the crusts off the tuna sandwiches I made earlier and arrange them like sailboats jamming together in a crowded harbor.

"I heard you and Dan broke up," I say, putting my boats in the fridge and turning back to the eggs. "I hope it wasn't because of what I said."

She keeps her head down and sweeps the broccoli crumbs from the cutting board into her hand. She walks them to the garbage can and brushes them in before saying, "I thought I told you I didn't want to talk about it."

"Sorry, I just … I wanted to clear the air. It seems silly."

"I asked you to leave me alone, okay?" Her years of practice being a misunderstood youth have served her well. She still won't look at me. Instead she clatters in the drawers for a vegetable peeler and then disappears into the back pantry for carrots.

I'm left in this basement kitchen cracking egg after egg on the long metal table. I roll each egg under my palm to loosen the shells and listen to Melissa shifting bags of vegetables and then the water running as she washes the carrots in the back sink.

She's gone a long time, and when she returns there's mascara smudged under her eyes, and she looks about five years older.

"I really care about you, Melissa," I say, flicking a tiny shell off one of the peeled eggs. "You've been my best friend for forever, and I don't want to lose that over something so stupid."

She's holding a dozen carrots in her hands, and water drips down her arms. She drops the carrots on the cutting board and keeps her face to them while she says, "You messed everything up for me," like we're on a bad soap opera.

She picks up a carrot and takes the peeler to it in long smooth strokes. Orange bits fly across the kitchen, and I half expect violin music to start playing and maybe a thunderstorm outside.

I accidentally drop the egg I'm peeling into the garbage can.

"I'm not sure I can be totally to blame," I say. "We were drunk. If Dan's going to react that badly to a meaningless kiss, then you two have got your own problems."

The carrot in Melissa's hand is peeled now, but she keeps going, almost mechanically, watching the carrot get thinner and thinner until it breaks and she drops it and the peeler on the table.

If this soap opera were any good, Dan would run in now with a set of conjoined twins from a previous love affair, or else Melissa would fall into a coma.

Instead she takes up the broken carrot and starts snapping it into smaller and smaller pieces. Her knuckles go white and she bites on her bottom lip so hard it starts to bleed.

"If you didn't want Dan to freak out," I tell her, dropping the peeled eggs into a bowl and barfing mayo over them. "Maybe you shouldn't have tried to make out with me in the first place."

And Melissa slams her hand on the table.

"Fuck." She says it rather than yells it, but her voice reverberates around us like we're inside an enormous bell. "You are so self-absorbed. It makes me want to punch you."

When she looks at me, her eyes are shining as though somewhere deep in her chest there is a forest, and the forest is on fire.

This is the Melissa I know. I've been waiting for her.

"All right," I say. "If it'll make you feel better, punch me."

Melissa licks the blood off her lip, and I set the bowl of eggs and mayo on the table and approach her, feeling something hot and blind rising inside of me.

"Knock out a few teeth," I tell her. "It'll add to your fucked-up tough-girl image. You obviously don't care about me anyway."

She stands her ground, and for a second I think she's going to do it. For a second I want her to do it, just so I can feel something, and maybe so I can hit her back.

"You're calling me self-absorbed?" I ask. I taste metal and sweat and months of frustration and disappointment pouring out of me. "You're the one who's blowing this out of proportion. You're the one who wrecked our whole last summer together. You're the one who's leaving."

The basement is too small and we are too big, and our voices are too loud.

"Don't start this with me, really."

And then she's gone. It's her feet on the stairs and the front door slamming, followed by a high-pitched ringing through the whole house. I bring my fist down so hard on the metal table that the bowl of egg salad falls on the floor. I kick it and it leaves a mayonnaise splatter across the oven.

Another mess courtesy of Melissa Desmond.

I finish the vegetable platter, organize the desserts, then start on the egg salad for a second time with the fight spinning through my head like it's on a merry-go-round. Maybe Melissa has changed. She's been acting so strange lately, maybe it is more than her just trying to act tough and tortured.

Luckily, though, with Melissa not here and Lincoln not here and Stephanie not here, there's not a lot of time to think about anything. After I finish these sandwiches I still have to make sixty-four mini-quiches and a fruit plate.

Before I know it, I'm wiping down the counters, and Tyler texts to say he'll pick me up in five minutes.

I turn off all the lights and stand still in the kitchen, listening to the clicks of the house settling and the highway in the distance. It's cloudy outside and cool and dark in here. I press my forehead against the metal table and feel my eyes closing. It feels like every day huge and important things are happening — earthquakes and political assassinations and suicide bombers — and then nothing changes. Cars drive back and forth across the highway. People are born. People die.

My phone rings and it's Tyler.

"I'm outside," he says. "I didn't want to ring the bell."

I take the bag I've packed with stolen sandwiches and desserts and meet him at his car.

"Not the best day for sunsets," he says while I put on my seatbelt and he backs out of the driveway. "If it doesn't work out, though, I have a plan B."

"Okay," I say. The windows are down and a cool breeze comes in. The sky is overcast, and it's definitely end-of-summer weather with autumn creeping in at the edges of the days.

"How was work?" Tyler asks.

"It was a weird day. Melissa came in for, like, thirty seconds, but otherwise it was just me which was kind of okay."

"So, as good as it can be," he says. "I worked in a kitchen for two years in Toronto, and it was horrible."

We drive onto the main street past a nail salon that changes its name every other week. Right now it's called Jenny Beauty Deluxe.

"Why was it so bad?" I ask.

"I realized I was a machine." He runs his fingers through his hair and glances at me as though he's checking to see if I'm listening. "They didn't really need me. Just my arms to chop things and mix salad dressing and whatever, and I was just a body attached to them."

"A cyborg."

"Yeah, exactly, and I would get so depressed talking to the people who had been there for a long time. They always seemed like they were waiting for it to get better or something. They would wait for their days off and then until

Christmas and then until summer, and it made me crazy because I mean what did they think was going to happen if they
kept doing everything the same? I didn't ever want to be like
them, but I worked there for two years somehow."

We're by the park now. The wind blows a plastic shopping
bag across the street in front of us and it catches in a tree.

"I don't know," I say. "I always thought it might be fun to be
a chef or something. You could invent your own recipes and
do taste tests and stuff."

"Yeah, but that's different. When I was working in the
kitchen all I did was cut vegetables. I just felt like I could be
doing so much more. I know it sounds cheesy but, like, look
at us. We're young, we're smart, we live in Canada, we could
actually do anything." We stop at a stop sign and he flicks the
pine-tree-shaped air freshener attached to the rearview mirror. It spins like a tiny tree in a tiny tornado.

"Even now, working at my uncle's shop," Tyler continues. "I
know it takes some skill to figure out what things are worth
and be hard with the customers and whatever, but every hour
I spend buying and selling other people's garbage makes me
work harder to finish school and save money. It would be so
easy to stay in Cavanaugh and work for my uncle and have
this just be my life, but I can't let that happen."

We stop at a set of traffic lights, and Tyler looks over at me
like he's just remembered I'm here.

"I guess I know what you mean," I say.

"I thought you would."

And we pull into the alley behind his uncle's shop.

"It's this way," Tyler says. He leads me up a metal fire escape
to two folding lawn chairs and a milk crate between them on
a gravel roof. I set the food on the crate and Tyler makes a

full circle, surveying the view like he's making sure it hasn't changed since he was up here last.

The building next door blocks out most of our view of the town, but on the other side we can see the west edge of Cavanaugh and beyond it farmers' fields that somehow look greener under the low gray sky.

"When I first moved to Cavanaugh I couldn't get over how much space there was," Tyler says. "You have to drive for an hour from Toronto before you reach a road that you can't see a subdivision from, but here there's just so much ... so much everything."

"See, it's not so bad here. I've only been to Toronto a few times and it just seemed so big and faceless." I take a seat on a lawn chair, and Tyler sits beside me with his feet kicked out and his face toward the fields.

"That's because you actually have to spend time there. You have to live in a neighborhood and get to know the little shops and the characters on the street. I have absolutely no idea what tourists do when they come."

I shrug.

"You said your mom grew up here, right?" Tyler asks with a bite of egg salad in his mouth. "Did she always live here, or did she move away and then come back?"

I don't really know what happened to my mother outside of Cavanaugh. She moved away when she was the same age I am now, but she and my grandma never got along. They kept in touch with Christmas cards and a phone call every six months. Even my dad dated her for less than half a year before they broke up and she moved somewhere new. He didn't even know she was pregnant with me until my grandma tracked him down almost seven years after I was born.

I only have one clear memory of my mother. I'm sitting on a kitchen counter somewhere, and she's painting my nails bright pink.

"Pretty," she kept saying. "You are so pretty …"

I look out at the rolling fields rolling away from us and listen to the cars on the highway somewhere behind us, and somewhere in the middle of everything, I remember that the earth is the biggest thing anyone has ever stood on.

"My mom moved away for a bit," I finally say. "I was born in Alberta, but we moved back when I was three."

"Are you guys close?"

The gray sky is slowly going a darker gray, and I picture the earth spinning around the sun and the sun a star in the Milky Way.

And when I look at Tyler he's looking right at me. His eyes are steady and dark and he looks at me like he knows who I am. He's found someone deep inside of me that I didn't even know about, and it's that look and the half-moon scar beside his left eye that makes me say, "My mom and I don't have a lot in common. She travels a lot for work so I don't see her too often."

"That's rough. I'm sorry."

"No, no, it's fine." But my voice seems too loud and too quick. "It's actually good. I … I see her every other week at least, but you know moms. It's nice to have my own space." And I stack two sandwich triangles on top of each other and shove them into my mouth so that I'll stop talking.

"Your parents are divorced, then?"

I put a third sandwich in my mouth and mumble something that kind of sounds like, "You know how it is." I'm not really lying. I'm not really saying yes or no. I'm doing a subtle half nod, and he can interpret it however he wants.

And then the wind picks up and the first few raindrops start to fall. They come down cold and hard like the nails holding the sky up are coming loose.

"It's okay. There's a plan B, remember?" Tyler says. He packs up the sandwiches and I follow him down the fire escape and through the pawnshop's back door.

"I'm actually a little happy that it rained," he says. "I set this up and I wasn't sure if we'd get to use it." He goes into the main shop in front of me and flicks on a few switches before he lets me through.

I squint, and it takes a second for my eyes to adjust to the lights that seem to be coming from everywhere all at once. I blink and I blink, and I see that Tyler has hooked up every old lamp in the store to extension cords, and they're all on. Blue shades, pink shades, green shades, there's light in every color, bouncing off the old plates, brass candlestick holders and mermaid figurines. Everything is alive like the entire store is an enchanted forest.

"Wow," I say.

Tyler leads me to a blanket on the floor lit up by a fiber-optic rose and what looks like a real turtle shell turned into a lamp.

"I hope it's not like too much or anything," he says. "Almost no one came into the shop today and, I don't know, I really like you and I thought it would be nice."

"It is nice," I say. "Now come here."

He's still standing above me with his hands in his pockets, but I pull him down to sitting, squeezed on the blanket between a shelf of old telephones and a three-foot-tall porcelain lion. I hold his hand and kiss the scar beside his eye.

"Thank you," I say. "This is great." And I kiss him on the lips.

He puts his hand on the base of my neck and holds me close with our lips still together. His skin is rough and warm as he slides his other hand down my chest to cup my right breast.

In the winter, Mark and I got drunk and made out at parties a few times while everyone else was passed out around us. It was exciting for a little while but then Mark got sick for almost a month. When he was well enough to party again, something didn't seem right, and we went back to being just friends like nothing else had ever happened.

Mark and I never went farther than where Tyler and I are right now, only Tyler is lifting the corner of my shirt and asking if he can take it off. I'm telling him yes and trying to look like I've done this before.

I let him run his hands over my body, and he smells like dirt in a forest and the rain on the roof. I kiss his neck and try to listen to my body and be calm.

I've got a few strands of Tyler's long dark hair in my mouth and his lips are on my ear and I'm trying to figure out if tonight will be the night I lose my virginity and if I should tell Tyler I haven't beforehand.

Tyler is kissing my neck again and I'm wondering how to hold my head and where my hands should go and if I'm a good kisser and if our kissing is compatible. I bring his mouth up to mine and wonder what will happen next.

Twenty minutes later we both have our shirts off but our pants are still on and my bra's still on. We lie an inch apart on the scratchy blanket on the pawnshop floor listening to the storm outside like something enormous trying to get in. A crack of thunder splits the sky, and the lamps flicker but then glow steady again.

I trace a circle around Tyler's bellybutton and say, "So, tell me about your family."

He exhales and cracks the knuckles on his left hand.

"There's just my sister, my parents and me," he says. "My parents are divorced, too."

"How was that?" I ask, and he shifts so he's propped up on his elbows.

"Honestly?"

I nod.

"It was really shitty." He brushes a hair away from my neck and traces my collarbone. "It's funny. I was fourteen, and I feel like it shouldn't have been so bad," he says. "I mean, I had my own life and everything, but I guess I just didn't see it coming." He looks at the ceiling as though he's trying to see the rain through the roof.

"Maybe it was just that it happened so fast," he continues. "Everything was fine and then suddenly my sister went away to college and my parents were fighting all the time. It was like everything I knew was all falling apart at once."

There's another crack of thunder, and he puts his arm around me and pulls me close with all the treasures in the pawnshop piled around us.

"I didn't really know how to deal with it," he says. "It wasn't just the divorce, obviously, but I started doing a lot of drugs."

Outside the rain is one million fingers against the roof, and the lights in the pawnshop flicker from the power surges and old extension cords.

"I dropped out of school and I was in rehab for a bit," he says. He kisses my shoulder and spins the number dial on an old-fashioned telephone to my right. "I felt like I couldn't hold onto anything and even if I could it didn't matter because it would all fall apart anyway." He lies on his back to stare at the ceiling. His hair spreads out around his head like each hair is a thought growing out of him.

"I don't know," he says. "It wasn't a good time."

There's something about Tyler's long mouth and his sad brown eyes stuck to the soggy roof that makes me remember one of the drives from Ontario to Alberta and back that I did with my dad. We were somewhere in the prairies looking at where whoever made the earth had gotten lazy with their sculpting and had pressed the land down flat and my dad said, "You know, people think that in Greek mythology Atlas carried the world on his shoulders, but it's not true. He actually carried the sky." We hadn't spoken for an hour before that and we didn't say anything for a long time after. We just looked out the window at the fields the color of long blond hair and the sky the biggest thing I'd ever seen …

Tyler sits up again and smiles at me and bites his thumb. He bites his thumb like he used to suck it when he was younger and still wants to.

"But things are a lot better now," he finally says. "For the first time ever, maybe, I'm really happy with where my life is going and I'm, like, excited for the future."

I put his hand in mine and flip it over to trace the tree tattooed onto his forearm. I put two fingers to his wrist like I learned to do in gym class, and we sit quietly while I check his pulse. It's strong and steady, and I imagine his veins like rivers, his blood rushing to his heart and back while we listen to the rain outside.

"Speaking of things getting kind of dark," Tyler says eventually. "I don't think you're supposed to bring up rehab on your third date." He shifts away from me and picks up the fiber-optic rose that's been changing colors this whole time.

"It's odd," he tells the rose. "I feel like I've known you for way longer than a week. I feel like I can trust you." He puts the rose back on the blanket and kisses my forehead and my neck and my shoulder.

"You should move to Toronto with me," he whispers into my hair. "We could be anyone we want to be."

And for a fraction of a second I can see it. We live above a bakery in Little Italy and buy all our groceries in Chinatown. On the weekends we go ice skating and to concerts in abandoned warehouses, and whatever happened in the past happened in a bad dream we almost forgot to wake up from.

When Tyler looks at me I try to make my face look blank and new like when we first met. All Tyler knew about me then was that I'm good at math and I like camping, and now he thinks my parents are divorced and my mom travels a lot for work, and that he can trust me.

12

The storm goes on all night, thunder and lightning and the rain trying to work its way through the window. I look at my clock every hour and I'm never sure if I'm sleeping or I'm awake.

I'm standing in the middle of a train station and everyone is staring at me. At first I can't figure out why, but then I realize my mouth is open and it's enormous. All my teeth are gold and I'm eating everything in sight. Newspapers, garbage cans. I take a bite the size of my head out of the wooden door that separates the station from the platforms. My stomach is a landfill and my mouth is a machine on overdrive. I chew and I chew, these gold teeth crashing against benches and suitcases and platform signs. I swallow everything down a throat like a long metal drainage pipe.

When a train pulls into the station, I start at the front and work my way toward the end car, tasting metal and blood and the passengers' cries before they're crushed between my golden jaws and swallowed into the darkness deep within my chest. Train car after train car gets erased by my enormous mouth, and there's nothing I can do but chew, and there's nothing anyone else can do but scream.

I wake to the dirty light of seven o'clock pressing through my window and a few raindrops landing outside. My dad is making coffee downstairs, and as always there's the highway like a hallway of white noise. I try to go back to sleep, but every time I do it's the same dream. Me eating train after train, my enormous mouth and gold teeth.

The box my grandma gave me is still in the back of my closet. I open it, and there are the teeth. Looking at them my mouth feels odd. I know it was a dream but I can still feel the gold in my gums and the train's engine grease on my tongue, and when I blink I can still see the horrified faces of the people I ate and hear their screams right before they disappeared into my mouth.

I drop the lid back down and am out the door without breakfast and without an umbrella less than a minute later. It's still raining like little stitches sewing the air together, but I walk fast with the box of teeth in the bottom of my bag as I make my way through the waking streets to my grandma's house.

My grandma is still asleep when I get there, so I let myself in and carry the box of teeth in front of me, looking for a place to hide them.

I'm not throwing them out. I'm just bringing them back to their home.

I trip over a toilet brush and an empty pack of chewing gum that have somehow found their way into the hallway, and I stumble into the living room where most of the stuff my grandma has collected has piled on top of itself like everything that's ever happened to her is still happening to her.

The Christmas tree with its rumpled branches is still set up in the corner, strangled by the lights we strung, and my Little Red Riding Hood Halloween costume is balled up on the windowsill.

I leave with the box of teeth still in my hand, hoping for air on the second floor.

My grandma is asleep in bed, wrapped in her old blue quilt with an extension cord, a hairspray bottle and a stapler tucked around her as though even when she's sleeping, all the things she can't get rid of still have their hold.

Farther down the hall is my old room. The walls are still yellow and the polka-dot curtains are still on the windows with spiderwebs stretching across them.

"Pick any color," my grandma said the summer I turned four. "This is your bedroom now. Let's make it a nice happy color."

For the first six months we called this my mother's room and I slept with my grandma in her bed ...

All my old stuff is still in here. The clothes I outgrew are in a pile on the floor, and my Prettiest Pony coloring book is on the dresser and almost hidden under the other things my grandma has collected over the years. On the bed there's a box of manila envelopes, three men's gym socks and a bicycle seat, and spread out across the floor are a bunch of old photographs, a stack of magazines, scissors and glue.

I sit on the carpet stained with paint and markers and years of dirty feet and take up the top photo on the pile.

It's my mother as a baby, held by my grandma's sister who died before I was born. Underneath it there's my school photo from kindergarten. I'd cut my hair myself the night before, and in the picture my bangs lie in a zigzag across my forehead.

It isn't until I'm almost through the photos in the first pile that I realize the ones in the second pile are different. There's a picture of a family cut out from a magazine, holding hands and walking on a beach somewhere, and under it there's my grandma and my mother in black-and-white, cut out from one photo and pasted on top of a green field with a maple tree and a blue sky. My mother looks about nine or ten in the cut-out picture. It must have been taken a few years before my grandfather got sick. Despite the careful cutting job, there's a man's hand on my grandma's right shoulder that couldn't be cut away.

I look up to remind myself where I am, my old peach bedspread and the picture of a sunset in a gold frame on the wall, and then I look down at the box of teeth I've still got in my lap.

The next picture on the pile makes me dizzy until I realize it's not me in a wedding dress but my grandma the same age I am now. She's staring at the camera with a look of total indifference. I've seen this photo before but now she's been cut from the church this picture was taken in and is waiting to be pasted somewhere new.

The floorboards shift in front of me, and my grandma is in the doorway looking down.

"Emily, what are you doing in here?" There's a stain on the front of her nightgown, a few brown spots dripped between blue flowers.

"I was … I was just looking at these pictures," I say, and I hand her the one of her in her wedding dress.

She stands in the doorway holding the photo for a long time. She looks at it like she's not really seeing the picture but the day the photo was taken, what the inside of the church looked like and what her father might have said before he walked her down the aisle. She uses her finger to trace the outline where the rest of the scene was cut away.

"I was pregnant here," she finally says, still looking at the picture. "Everyone thought I would have a baby, but it turned out to be a bright red butterfly, and it flew away."

She always talks about her past like this, her baby was a butterfly and her husband was a bear. From what I've figured out, my great-grandfather was the head of some type of church, and when he found out my grandma was pregnant, he made my grandfather marry her. A few months later she miscarried and couldn't get pregnant again until they'd almost stopped trying twelve years later.

My grandma lets the cut-out picture drop to the carpet and brushes the long gray hair out of her eyes.

"That was all a long time ago," she tells me, and she uses her toe to shift the pictures so the one of her in the dress is hidden under the others. She stares down at the photos spread across the carpet like she's staring into the bottom of a well, and I'm not sure how to pull her back to reality.

"Here," I say. "Let me put these away."

She watches me like she's watching a television screen as I slide the photographs into a more organized pile and stack them with the magazines, scissors and glue. I slip the square box with the gold-capped teeth into the pile, too, and tuck everything into the back shelf of my old closet.

I lead my grandma to the kitchen and open all the windows so that fresh air blows through. It stirs the pages on a stack of newspapers near the sink, and I put a plate on them so they don't blow away.

"Are you hungry?" I ask her.

"A little," she says, but she still seems lost somewhere between that girl in the wedding dress and the seventy-five-year-old woman sitting at the kitchen table now.

I make eggs and toast and tea and tell her about Tyler and how he lit up every light in the pawnshop for me last night.

"He's really serious," I say. "But it's kind of nice. I feel like he actually listens to all the stuff I say."

I try to keep talking while I cook so there isn't any space left in the kitchen for the past to get in.

Just as I'm setting the table, my grandma goes to the garden and comes back with a purple flower. She puts it in a rinsed-out jam jar as a centerpiece.

"I've been adding coffee grounds to my soil," she tells me as we eat. "I read it in a book once, but I can't remember why they said to do it."

She uses her toast to wipe the runny egg off her plate and washes it down with a sip of tea.

"Maybe the caffeine makes the flowers perky," she says, and then she laughs.

She takes the flower out of the jar and smells it, then offers it to me.

"Do you smell coffee?" she asks.

I tell her I don't.

"Me, neither." And she stands to clear the plates away.

"I wonder if growing your plants in different soils makes them smell different," she says. "The older I get the more it seems I have to learn. Sometimes you just have to try your best with what you know, though, and hope it works out."

13

I'm on my way home from breakfast with my grandma when a car slows beside me. I don't look up until Robert honks the horn and shouts my name.

"You need a ride somewhere?" His eyes look closer together and his cheeks look bigger when he grins.

I glance at the road ahead and the clouds that might open again at any second, and I climb into the passenger seat. Robert's green grocery-store vest is bunched up on the floor beside an open bag of chips.

"Like my car?" he asks. It's a boxy beige thing with a hole in the dashboard like someone ate the radio out.

"Yeah, it's nice."

"There's no A/C or anything yet, but there will be." He speeds forward after a stop sign and makes a sharp turn down a side street.

"I just picked it up last night before work from this guy up north," he says. "And this is just the first thing."

We stop at another stop sign and the glove compartment's mouth drops open. It's more amazed than I am.

"The first thing?" I ask.

"I mean, you know Melissa with her huge scholarship and all, after I stopped with hockey she sort of became the poster child for our family. It's great for her that my parents are so proud, but I'm her brother. I'm her older brother."

"Okay," I say. The glove compartment opens again. I jam it closed and take a handful of chips from the bag at my feet.

"Well, everyone thinks I'm not as smart as her," Robert continues. "I smoke a lot of weed and I had all those concussions and whatever else, and maybe I'm not as smart as her, but that doesn't mean I'm nothing, you know?"

"I think so."

"I have these goals. No one thinks I can do anything anymore, but look, I bought this car. I haven't smoked up in five days. No, six now. Six days."

"Oh, that's great," I say, and Robert slows down for a squirrel standing paralyzed in the middle of the road.

"Yeah, it is great. Thank you. No one's said that yet, but it is great. I mean, look. Here is a real-life car that I bought with my own money." He flicks the headlights on and off, but it's daytime so we can't tell if they work.

"You should paint it," I say.

"Yeah? What color?"

"Bright green."

"Green like money," he nods.

"Exactly."

Robert turns the corner into our neighborhood. The houses here are just one house on repeat, and I don't remember which house is supposed to be mine.

"Or black like black ice," Robert says. He stops in front of a house like all the others and I imagine myself walking into it, reading my book on black holes and having a snack, waiting until the afternoon when I have to go to work, and after work waiting until it's dark outside and I can go to bed.

"You did want to go home, right?" Robert asks.

"I don't have to," I say.

"Oh, really?" He takes a handful of chips from the bag at his side, and I take some more as well.

"Well, I was just going to drive around for a bit, see how the car handles."

"Cool," I say. "Let's do it."

He starts the car again. I roll down the window and watch the gingerbread houses flip past us. The houses are siblings in a family band. They sing Christian folk songs and have abusive stage parents who make them all wear matching clothes.

"Okay," I say after another handful of chips. "Show me your parallel parking, right up here."

"Behind this van?"

"Yeah, I want to see."

"God, I haven't done this since my driving test. You have to be chill, okay?"

I nod and he pulls up beside the van and shifts into reverse.

"My dad was the worst for freaking out," he says. "It sounds so stupid, but he actually made me cry one time."

"What happened?"

He turns the wheel and backs up slowly. I press my back to my seat and try to make myself the color of the upholstery.

"Have you ever seen my dad when he gets angry, like really angry and throws shit?"

Four years ago I went to hang out with Melissa one day and something felt off about her house as soon as I walked in.

The air was too thick and there wasn't enough of it. Melissa was alone, and there was an empty space in her living room where their glass coffee table had been.

Something about the way she held her bottom lip between her teeth told me I'd better not ask what had happened.

"My dad broke the table," Melissa said later when we were dyeing her hair in the bathtub. "And I peed in the milk." She said it the same way you might say, *I hear they're opening up a new restaurant by the movie theater.*

"Is that why your dad broke the table?" I asked.

"No, he broke the table last night, and I peed in the milk this morning as revenge."

And then she stuck her head under the bathtub tap to wash the dye out like there was nothing else left to say …

Robert is still looking at me and I shrug.

"I don't know," I say. "Maybe not like the full deal."

He nods.

"We were on this back road in the middle of nowhere," he says. "And my dad started screaming at me. I don't even remember what I did wrong, but he started punching the dashboard, and I thought he would crack it or break his hand or something — shit." Robert hits the curb and pulls out to try the parallel park again.

"My dad kept yelling all this really vicious shit at me. Shit I don't even want to repeat, and so I just stopped the car in the middle of the road. I took the keys and I walked out." He straightens the car behind the van and I open the passenger door. We're about two and a half feet from the curb. I shake my head.

"Fuck," Robert says, and he pulls out again.

"What happened after?" I ask.

"Well, he couldn't go anywhere. I had the keys so he couldn't drive off. I walked down the road and left him in the car screaming. I had my lighter and I just started burning shit — twigs and leaves and stuff until I ran out of lighter fluid. Later my dad found me and drove us home." He backs in a third time. He hits the curb but keeps driving.

"He's an all-right guy, though, my dad. He just has these anger problems sometimes, and I can't always handle it."

"I don't know if that's your job," I say. "To handle it." I open the car door and examine the wheel chewing up the wet grass.

"Let's go on the highway," Robert says. "Let's drive fast." He goes thirty over the speed limit, around the overpass and out of Cavanaugh. Sun breaks through the thick oatmeal sky and makes the farms we pass seem drawn by little kids. There are red barns and bright green fields, and we're going so fast that even the cows seem like white blobs with black splotches balanced on four stick legs.

Now that we're on the highway there's not a lot for Robert and me to talk about. I've known him my whole life, but he's always just been Melissa's older brother. He used to play hockey when he was in high school. He was being scouted for the OHL and everything, but he got too many concussions and had to stop.

"Let's go here," I say when I see the sign to Renner Lake. "My dad used to take me fishing here, but we haven't been in a long time."

Robert follows the signs and we end up in a gravel parking lot at the edge of a deserted lake. We are the first people on earth and this is the first lake we have ever seen. There's a dock and a rocky beach, and we don't know what to call it, so we call it Renner Lake.

My shoes slip on the slimy rocks on the walk to the water, and I have to grab onto Robert's shoulder to keep from falling. I take my shoes off and throw them back toward the car. There's broken green glass between the rocks, but this is a time before disease and before injuries.

Robert's pants have some sort of red sauce spilled on them from his all-night shift at the grocery store, and I'm barefoot in the shirt I slept in and an old pair of jeans. We stand together at the edge of the lake like we're in some photo shoot for ugly people. The clear lake reflects us and the spruce trees behind us, and I'm not sure which version of us is underwater and which is on the surface looking down.

Robert picks up a rock the size of a baseball and throws it into the lake. The water swallows it with a gulp, and we watch ripples cut across the surface.

I pick up a rock and throw it as hard as I can as far as I can. It makes a splash that looks higher than the trees on the other side of the lake. I wait for the water to settle, then pick up another rock and throw it even harder and even farther.

Robert throws a rock and I throw a rock. We throw more and more. I don't know what we're throwing rocks for, but we throw them like we're trying to clear the shore or flood the lake. We are the first people, and we want our beach to be clean and new. We throw and we throw, not waiting to watch one rock land before we grab the next. We want all the rocks in the water. All the rocks along the shore and all the gravel from the parking lot. We want to be the only things on earth.

All we hear is splashing, and all we see are the ripples in the water. The rocks go flying and our hands go with them. Our hands are birds and we are birds and we soar above the lake with each stone and are dunked under. We're being baptized again and again.

We end up sitting on rocks too big to throw. Robert and I are both covered in mud with a mud circle all around us where the rocks we threw in used to be. We watch the lake until the last ripple is absorbed by the cedars. The ripples in the water become the rings in the trees, another ring for every year.

A dog comes out of the woods on the other side of the lake. It barks at us but we can't understand what it's saying. We are the first people, and this is the first dog, and this is the first day, and already we're separate from the rest of nature.

Without saying anything, we both know that it's time to go back.

"Listen," I say when we're almost at my house. "You shouldn't be this nice to me. I was never nice to you, and a few weeks ago at that party, what I said — "

Robert holds up his hand with his eyes still on the road.

"I know," he says.

"Then why are you?"

He sighs and picks at a sticker gumming up the steering wheel.

"Just in case," he says.

But I can only blink at him as he turns onto my street.

"Two years ago I finished high school, and all my friends moved away, and it was really shitty. It was like I didn't really realize what was going to happen, and then all of a sudden I was the only one left in Cavanaugh."

"Oh," I say. "Okay."

He pulls into my driveway, but I don't get out of the car.

"I know Melissa's pissed at you," he says. "But she's leaving on Thursday, and two days before my best friend moved away it would have been nice to have someone say, 'Hey, there's nothing wrong with you. If you need a little more time to figure your shit out, that's okay.' So here I am."

"Oh," I say. "Thank you."

I've known Robert for so long that I've forgotten what he really looks like. I guess I always figured he'd look the same, but when I look at him now I can tell he's older. There's something about his eyes. His back is straighter and he tilts his chin farther down. He doesn't look like a hockey player anymore, just a guy who works at the grocery store and likes to drive around town.

"This was fun," I tell him. "I'm sorry again for, you know, being such an asshole before."

He nods and salutes as I get out of the car.

I walk to my porch, but then stand and watch him adjust his rearview mirror and put the car into reverse. It's another thing I feel I should always remember, this moment and how Robert looks. I don't know why, but it seems important to me to always have this picture, my best friend's older brother sitting in the car he's going to paint green for money or black for black ice, and how his face looked so serious, like a face in a painting, when he said, *There's nothing wrong with you. If you need a little more time to figure your shit out, that's okay.*

He frowns and rubs a smudge off his side mirror. It makes him look like Melissa for a second, until he notices I'm still watching. Then he smiles and drives away.

When I get inside, my house feels abandoned. It's cool and empty like we built it at the bottom of the ocean. My dad has already left for the day, and we never got around to hanging pictures on any of the walls.

I walk along the hallway feeling the white space and looking for cracks in the paint where the sound of the highway is getting in, but it all seems sealed up tight. There are secret speakers under the carpet and in the rafters that play the sound of cars driving all day and all night.

There's a note on the kitchen table:

Em,

That conference in Montreal is in two weeks. I've booked a room with two beds in case you'd like to come along, but please let me know either way.

Dad

He's left the hotel brochure as well as printed-out information on a few of the schools he was telling me about. Small Business Management sounds like something you'd make kids in juvie take as a cruel and unusual form of punishment, but the culinary schools actually sound kind of fun. The class list includes Properties of Food, Changing Flavor Trends and Contemporary Pastry Designs.

I imagine a teacher with a French accent and an elaborate scarf going, "Horseradish and chocolate is very trendy right now. Peanut butter and bacon is so last season." Or else, "Today in Contemporary Pastry Design we will be making minimalist creampuffs. It is more about the idea of the puff than the actual pastry."

But then I imagine the seven-hour car ride there with my dad while he talks about the effects of global warming on mollusks and I rip out my arm hairs one at a time to keep from dying of boredom.

Then again, going to Montreal with my dad when I was

ten wasn't actually that bad. It was the only trip we took that wasn't camping or else to Alberta to visit my grandparents.

My dad had reconnected with an ex-girlfriend from university. She was living in Boston with her daughter who was a year older than me, and the plan was that the four of us would meet in Montreal and spend a week together.

I don't know what happened exactly, but the woman canceled at the last minute. My dad had already paid for the hotel and taken time off work, so he and I ended up going anyway. It was the middle of a heatwave, and my dad was too disappointed to make any plans, so we spent the week eating ice cream in parks and watching people go by. We translated their French into ridiculous conversations and made up stories about who they were and where they were going. It was like with people speaking a different language all around us, we were finally able to understand each other ...

I leave the information about Small Business Management as well as the note and the brochure on the kitchen table, but take the list of culinary courses to my room before getting ready for work.

14

The next day I go to Tyler's for lunch. He makes garlic bread and I make salad like we're married.

The kitchen is maroon, and there are loon pictures and woodcarvings on all of the walls. The end-of-summer sun comes through the open window, and Tyler's uncle's golden retriever is in the backyard gnawing on a stick twice as big as its body.

"Wait," says Tyler. "We need music." He slides the garlic bread into the oven and disappears into the living room.

"Check this out," he says, coming back with a record. On the front there's a woman wearing a gray turban with a pink feather as big as an entire bird sticking out the top.

"Do you know Bessie Smith?"

I shake my head.

"This is my uncle's, but my dad has the same record." Tyler disappears back into the living room. There's static, then a woman's voice like out of a megaphone starts to sing.

"My dad will only ever play this in the summer," Tyler tells me. "He has a whole list of what kind of music you should listen to each season."

Tyler comes back into the kitchen. He puts his hands on my hips from behind and sways. The music is blues, I guess, but old like we dug up a tin can from a hundred years ago. When we opened the can, this song came out.

"*Trouble, trouble, I've had it all my days,*" the singer sings, and Tyler sings along.

I spin so I'm facing him and put my hands on his waist with our bodies almost touching.

"*… the day you quit me, honey, it's coming home to you.*"

Tyler and I turn our bodies around and around the kitchen. He pulls me tighter into him until our chests are pressed together and the loud sad music surrounds us like a warm sad cloud. It's one song and then another with the words on a long red rope winding us together.

I put my ear to Tyler's chest and feel his lungs shift with every breath and his heart beating the blood through his body. His voice is just a whisper, like something he can't control coming out of him, "*That man I hate to lose. That's why momma's got the blues.*"

A cool breeze comes from the open window to counteract the heat of our bodies and the heat of the music, and we only break apart when we smell the garlic bread burning.

"Shit," Tyler says, opening the oven and waving the smoke away, and then the smoke detector goes off and I'm waving a tea towel in front of it while Tyler pulls the burning garlic bread out of the oven with his bare hands and throws it onto the bare table.

"That was dramatic," he says as the smoke clears. He sucks on his fingers and examines where the tips were burnt by the bread. I go back to the salad and he runs his fingers under the tap, and the music in the other room goes on as though nothing happened.

After lunch, Tyler takes me on a tour of the house and we end up in his bedroom. It's in the basement, and he has to duck to get down the stairs. Hopefully he's stopped growing, because if he were half an inch taller, his head would hit the ceiling.

The basement is pretty big, though. It's damp and the walls are thick like we're in an emptied-out swimming pool. There's an armchair, a desk, a little TV and a guitar in here as well as a crumpled Salvador Dali poster on the wall. Tyler's bed is a pullout couch with sheets the color of green pool sludge.

"It's messy," Tyler says, and he picks up a pile of clothes hanging off an abandoned treadmill in the corner of the room. He stands looking down at them for a second, lost as to where to put them, then shoves everything into one of his open desk drawers.

"Oh, look at this." He takes something metal out of a second drawer and brings it to the pullout.

The hinges creak when I sit down beside him.

"It's my great-grandfather's compass." He flips the lid open to show a crack in the glass and a little arrow balancing underneath. Tyler twists the compass back and forth to show how the arrow holds its position, and we sit for a minute, mesmerized.

We let the dog in after lunch, and the only sound other than the faint hum of the highway is its nails on the tile floor upstairs.

"Who was he?" I ask.

"My great-grandfather? I actually don't know anything about him." And one corner of Tyler's mouth pulls up to show his crooked teeth. "This might sound kind of … well, I've basically told you everything about me now so …"

He brings the compass close to his face and squints at it, then flips it over like he's expecting an answer to be engraved on the back.

"I kind of like not knowing," he finally says. "I think he was just this dude living his life. But at the same time, so many of his choices probably had a huge effect on whether I'd even be born."

He opens the compass again and hands it to me. The metal is warm on my palm, and the crack in the glass looks like a tree growing across the surface.

"It freaks me out, but in a good way," Tyler says. "There are so many directions you can go, and no matter what you choose it's going to have an effect on everything else."

The compass has an odd metallic smell mixing with the sweat from my palm and the smell of Tyler's cologne. His shoulder is touching mine, and he puts his hand on my knee.

"But then how do you decide anything?" I ask. I try to focus on the compass in my hand and not on Tyler's hand sliding up my thigh and around to my lower back.

"You just go for it, I guess." He puts his hand on top of mine and closes the compass. He takes it back to the desk drawer, then stands in front of me and pushes the limp hair from my face. His hands are warm, and when he kisses me he's breathing hard and nervous, and I kiss him back, feeling like my heart is made of nuts and bolts inside my chest.

I lie back on the bed and Tyler is on top of me. The only sound is our breathing and the highway and the dog upstairs. Tyler's mom and aunt will be in Toronto until dinner, and his uncle will be at the pawnshop until later tonight.

"Can I take this off?" Tyler asks, tugging at the bottom of my shirt.

I nod, and he takes his shirt off, too. His skin is salty and warm, and my chest is a magnet pressing my body into his. His fingers run though my hair, and his lips are on my neck.

And now my bra is coming off. Tyler fumbles with the clip while my hips grind into his, and the pullout moans beneath us.

I guess I always thought I'd lose my virginity like this. Melissa's cousin Darlene used to talk about a feather bed and roses and candlelight, but Melissa lost hers to her first boyfriend three years ago in the tube slide at the park. Now that I'm here in Tyler's damp basement, I'm not surprised.

Tyler asks if he can take my pants off, and all I have to do is follow his lead. Soon I will be having sex. I will be the type of person who has sex with other people.

With one hand Tyler rubs over my underwear, and with the other he guides my hand down to his boxers, and I remember that people don't just have sex to brag to their friends or to check off on their bucket list. People have sex because it feels good. His body and my body and the sweat on our skin.

We're down to our underwear now with two thin layers of cotton between us, and I roll on top of him and kiss his chest and leave a red mark on his neck.

I push my hair out of my face and my tongue in his mouth because I am a part of this, too. And when Tyler hooks his thumb under the elastic of my underwear and asks if they should come off, I'm out of breath and electric with his warm strong hands on my skin, and my body on top of his.

"Not yet," I tell him. "This is so good as it is."

"Oh," he says. "Of course." He goes back to kissing me, and I run my fingers down his side.

After a long time we roll away from each other. We lie face up on the pullout still in our underwear and stare at the ceiling with the light coming in blue from the low window.

"I forgot to tell you," Tyler says, pulling himself to sitting. "I got into a night-school program."

"Oh, cool," I say.

There are three pimples on Tyler's back, and I draw a line from one to the other like I'm making a new constellation.

"Yeah, I'm going to get to finish my last few high-school courses by Christmas." He rolls his shoulders against my finger, and the hinges on the pullout creak as he flops back down on his side. "I've already started looking for jobs and places in Toronto available January first."

"January first?"

"I wish it was sooner, but I can't afford Toronto rent without working full time."

I reach my hand to touch the scar on the side of his face. It's smooth, and I trace my finger along it like I'm trying to make a memory of the memory of whatever violence happened to him to get that scar.

"That's so exciting," I finally say, but I'm not sure if it sounds genuine.

"I wasn't joking when I said you should come," he tells me. "We wouldn't have to move in together or anything, but it would be cool to have you there."

I move my finger back and forth along the scar again, then trace his eyebrows down his nose to his thin lips and up around his ear, but I suddenly feel like I'm in a movie. We're hired actors, and when the shoot finishes we'll never see each other again. Tyler will go back to Toronto, and I will be left in Cavanaugh. We'll both play other parts in other movies, and our great-grandchildren will never even know we met.

"That sounds like fun," I say.

"Really?"

"I don't know, maybe. I don't really know what I'm doing here."

Tyler wraps his arms around me and leans his head on my chest, but I still feel very small and very young because nineteen years ago I didn't exist, and in a few months from now Tyler will be gone and he won't even remember I'm still here.

"I should go," I tell Tyler. "I said I'd help my grandma with some things around the house this afternoon."

"Really?"

"Yes," I say, only I don't know why I'm saying it. I just want to be alone all of a sudden, although as soon as I am alone, walking the forty-five minutes back to my house, I wish I hadn't left.

Lincoln's only been gone three days, but I come home to find a postcard from him in the mailbox. At first I'm amazed by the speed of the postal service until I see the picture is the Toronto skyline with an obnoxious maple leaf photoshopped behind it.

Emily,

I'm having a great trip so far. Pearson International Airport is an exotic and glamorous place. I hope I never have to leave. Wish you were here!

Lincoln

I groan and tack the postcard to the bulletin board in my room.

I started a message to him last night, but all I have written is —

Dear Lincoln,

Today at work I spilled milk all over my pants. I had to spend the whole day in them, and I'm pretty sure the milk was starting to go bad.

If this keeps up I'll have to start inventing things so he doesn't start thinking he was the only interesting part of my life.

15

It's only been a few hours since I saw Tyler, but he looks different, cracking his knuckles in my front hall. He's wearing a black hoodie and dark jeans, and his hair is loose behind him. It's dark out now, and the sound of my dad watching TV in the basement echoes up at us.

"Hey, what's up?" I say. I go on my tiptoes to kiss his cheek, but he turns his head away.

"Is there somewhere we can go to talk?" he asks.

"There's the park down the street," I say.

I slide on my shoes and then pause.

"Is it cold out?"

"Yeah, a little," Tyler says.

Outside I go to link arms with him, but his body stays stiff. I put my hands in my pockets and try to keep up with his quick pace.

"So, what's going on?" I ask. I'm a little out of breath, but I don't know if it's from how fast we're walking or Tyler's stiff arms and dark eyes.

Tyler breathes out hard and runs his fingers through his hair.

"I needed to talk to you."

When we get to the park I sit on a bench in the playground, but Tyler stays standing. He kicks the gravel beneath his feet like he's trying to kick away the bits of the world he doesn't like.

"I've been hearing some things." He speaks as though he's pulling the words from somewhere deep inside his chest one at a time. "And I didn't think they were true because it's not what you said, but I was talking with my aunt about you, and you know, were you lying to me?" He kicks the stones again, and it feels as though they've landed in my stomach.

"What do you mean?" I shift on the bench but I can't seem to find a way to sit without my bones digging into the plastic and the plastic digging into my bones.

"I told my aunt I was going out with you, and she said she knew who you were."

I don't look up. There's a used Band-Aid mixed in with the gravel at my feet, and I feel it inside me, too.

"Okay," I finally say. But it feels like we're in a movie again, and I already know the ending. Something bad's about to happen, but the script has already been written.

"And maybe my aunt is wrong," Tyler continues. "Maybe there are two Emily Robinsons in Cavanaugh or she got the name wrong or something, but she was sure it was you." He looks at me, but I look at the ground because I have no idea what I'm supposed to say.

"My aunt didn't say a lot," Tyler says. "I don't know what she was referring to, but ... but was it a lie, Emily? All that stuff about your parents being divorced and your mom traveling a lot for work?"

I take a deep breath in and a deep breath out, but it doesn't loosen the gravel and dirt and used-up Band-Aids I've somehow sucked into my stomach. I still can't look at Tyler so I look past the swings and the slide to the chain-link fence at the edge of the park and the highway beyond it. The cars' headlights are mechanical eyes boring into the night.

"I told you things I've never told anyone before, and the whole time you were lying to me?" He goes to crack his knuckles but no sound comes out. He bites his thumb and looks at me and follows my line of sight to look at the highway behind him.

We're both still for a minute, watching cars drive from places I've never been to places I'll never go.

"Well?" Tyler finally says, and when I look at him he looks miles and miles away. I look down at my hands and I feel like I have blood on me. I'm in junior high all over again, and everyone is looking at me and everyone is thinking *Suicide Baby*. There's blood under my fingernails and behind my ears that will never wash away.

"That story ruins everything," I tell the highway and the cars. "Even now, it's ruining this. It's ruining my whole life."

"I thought we had a connection," Tyler says. "But it's like you were just trying to see what secrets you could get out of me."

"That's not it," I say. "I just wanted you to get to know the real me."

"So you lied to me about your entire life?"

A man and a woman have brought their dog to the park to play, but as soon as they come close enough to hear the tone of our conversation, they veer to the far edge of the field near the fence and the highway.

"No, that's the thing," I finally manage to say. "It's not my entire life. It's just this one thing, and it's not who I am. It doesn't even matter."

Tyler leans on a fire pole at the edge of the playground and makes a little hill of gravel with his feet. He steps on the hill, and the gravel spreads in every direction.

"All that stuff about my parents' divorce, how it was hard and the drugs and whatever. I wouldn't have told you if … I mean, I thought we'd been through the same things."

I've twisted two pieces of hair under my chin. I spin them around and around until they pull on the roots and a few tiny hairs rip out. I do it just so I can feel something and realize this is real, but when I look at Tyler he still seems far away.

"I never specifically said my parents were divorced," I say. "I mean, you asked me if they were, and I think I just said, 'You know how it is.' And you interpreted it to mean yes."

"What?" he asks.

I look down at his hands. They're illuminated and yellow in the yellow park light, and they're shaking. He shakes them out and tries to hold them steady again, but they're moving on their own.

"You can't," he says. "You can't argue this on semantics. All that stuff about you and your mom not getting along, and how she travels a lot for work? That's just my interpretation?"

"Well, that was … that was different. I mean, no one gets along with their mom," I say, but my voice sounds like a squeak out of a helium balloon.

"That's not the issue," Tyler says. "You manipulated me into telling you all this really personal stuff and you're not even going to admit it was wrong?"

He seems exhausted all of a sudden. He leans back against the fire pole again and slides down until he lands in the gravel and the dirt and the used Band-Aids and cigarette filters. When he looks up at me, his face is the moon.

"This isn't how I thought this conversation would go," he says. He's clasped his hands together to keep them still, and his voice is quiet and disappointed. "I thought we would come out here and talk about everything, and it would all be some big misunderstanding. I didn't know a person could be like that."

I open my mouth to speak but no words come out.

"The worst part is I don't think you even realize how shitty this is." He shifts the gravel around him like he's going to bury himself in it.

"It's complicated, though," I say. "I mean nothing is ever really one thing, is it?" But I don't know what I'm saying.

Tyler wipes his hands covered in gravel dirt on his pants and then looks at me with the last rays of hope slowly leaving his sad brown eyes.

"Okay," he says. "Go on."

Only I don't know what to say.

"I don't know," I say.

He uses the fire pole to help him stand, as though he's suddenly become unbelievably old.

"I just feel so stupid," he says. "I mean, Neil warned me to be careful. He hinted there was something wrong with you. I can't believe I fell for it."

Tyler holds his hands in front of him. He looks at me and then at the sky and then down at his hands as though he thought he was holding something and it's only now that he's realizing he wasn't.

"I guess I'll go," he says. He pulls his hood up and walks away slowly, as though even now he's listening for me to call him back and tell him what he wants to hear.

I don't know what to say, though. His body is a black

outline getting smaller and smaller, and I don't know what I'm supposed to do.

It's cold now, but I've been frozen to this bench watching the cars on the highway beyond the fence. I don't know what time it is or where these cars are going so late at night, but I watch them until my bones are as stiff as coat hangers, and then I will myself toward the washroom at the far edge of the park. It's supposed to be locked at night, but the park staff never want to walk this far in the dark, so it's usually open.

The mirror is cracked, and in my reflection the parts of my face won't fit together properly.

Maybe everyone in town was right all along — all the people who said there must be something wrong with me, that what my mother did couldn't possibly have left me normal, that something inside of me has gone horribly wrong. I was the only one who didn't notice I was different, and now it's too late.

I think of the picture tucked in the back of my old closet at my grandma's house, the one of my mother and my grandma looking blankly into the camera, how they were cut out from a black-and-white photo and glued onto a green field with a blue sky behind them. I remember how their faces looked, how they stared into the camera as though they already knew what was going to happen to them. My mother was only nine or ten in the photo, but it was like she already knew she was going to end up in a bathtub of her own blood and everyone in her home town talking about it forever. And my grandma looked like she knew she would end up alone in an old house slowly suffocated by all the things she can't seem to get rid of. In the picture there was a large gray hand on my grandma's shoulder that couldn't be cut away.

It was stupid of me to think I could ever escape, that I could ever be normal and live a happy life with these people that came before me.

I look at myself in the broken mirror now, hiding out in this damp bathroom with the highway sound coming through the open window and the white light flickering above, and I ask my cut-up reflection, *Do I look sad? Do I look like terrible things have happened to me?*

But the girl in the mirror looks normal. She's got brown hair and green eyes and a wide nose, and she looks like someone who's good at math and likes to cook and go camping and fishing. She looks like the kind of girl whose dad took her to the zoo when she was eleven and out of all the people there, she was the one who was picked to help feed the elephants. She looks like when she was eleven she got to touch a real live elephant, and its skin was tough and thick and full of coarse hairs. Even as she was doing it, she could hardly believe that she was there, that of all the people at the zoo, she had been chosen. That once in her life she had been the lucky one.

I use the toilet and read the graffiti on the stall walls, *K+R Forever* and a drawing of a leprechaun.

And in pencil near the toilet-paper dispenser, someone has written, *Melissa Desmond is a dyke.*

Without even thinking about it I lick my thumb and rub the letters out, but the lead leaves a gray mark on the wall and a gray mark on my skin, and I remember Melissa standing in my bathroom mirror last winter and asking, "What do you think I would look like if I was a lesbian?"

She'd shown up at my house twenty minutes earlier with ripped jeans and a bleeding lip and her left eye swelling. It was the middle of February and there was road salt and gravel stuck into the cut on her knee. She wasn't wearing a coat and her hands were curled into fists, either crippled from the cold or still ready to fight someone.

I looked at her in my doorway, all blood and cold and her hard brown eyes glazed over and electric. All I could think of was that little kid's rhyme, *All the king's horses and all the king's men couldn't put Humpty together again.*

But then Melissa smiled. Her bloody mouth showed bloody teeth, and her eyes changed back to the Melissa I'd known my whole life.

"Well, can I come in or should we just stand here?" she asked.

I moved to the side and watched her kick her boots by the door and disappear into the kitchen. I found her in there sitting on the table and eating the peanut butter toast I'd just made for myself. Her hair was tangled and enormous, and the skin around her eye was already starting to bruise.

"This just tastes like blood," she said. She swung her feet under the table and scratched a bit of dried blood off her cheek.

"Well, maybe we should, you know, fix some of this," I said, pointing to her knee and her mouth and her eye.

"Why? Do I have something in my teeth?" She spread her lips to show me her bloody mouth but winced with pain.

"Okay, I get it. You're funny," I said. "Now come with me." I led her to the bathroom and made her take her jeans off and sit at the edge of the tub, but she was so banged up I didn't know where to start. I got some ice for her eye and began working the gravel out of her cut-up knee. I kept splashing water on my pants, and I ended up taking my jeans off, too.

"This homoerotic situation isn't really helping my case," Melissa said, gesturing to her bare legs and my bare legs and me leaning over her.

"What do you mean?" I asked. Her hands were still in fists, but it wasn't from the cold anymore.

"You know how Brad Pelletier used to date Estelle?" she asked. "Well, Brad's been telling everyone they broke up because Estelle and I hooked up at Neil's New Year's party." She winced as I splashed more warm water over her cut-up knee. She and Estelle disappeared for almost an hour during that party, and Estelle left crying later that night, but Estelle has always been a drama queen, and I never thought one thing had to do with the other.

"Estelle and I were just talking, though," Melissa said. "And so I beat Brad up. Or at least I tried to." She looked down at her right hand still curled in a fist. Her fingers were starting to swell, and one of them was resting at an odd angle.

"Why?" I asked.

"Because fuck him. Fuck all these people and their stupid rumors."

I put a bandage over Melissa's knee and stood looking at her still so cut up and angry, checking her hand to see how many fingers were broken.

"People will grab hold of anything," I told her. "Remember when we all thought Mr. Butler was born with his knees facing the wrong way, and he was disqualified from the Olympics because he ran all the races backward?"

Her chin gets a dimple in it when she frowns, but from that angle it looked more like a scar. It was a scar she'd been born with, left over from something terrible that had happened in a previous life.

"Didn't you start that rumor?" she asked.

"Yeah, but everyone believed it."

I went to get us pants and when I came back, Melissa was standing in front of the medicine-cabinet mirror, examining the cut in her lip.

"I think the worst thing about being gay would be that you'd have to be gay forever," she said to her reflection. "I mean, you couldn't be gay and then still have a husband and kids and all the things you've always wanted."

"You could buy sperm or something," I said, holding up the pants for her. She looked over at me like she didn't realize I was standing there and that she was saying those thoughts out loud.

"Maybe," she shrugged. "It wouldn't be the same, though."

"I guess," I said. "But look at me or, like, Mark's family. Even you had your grandpa living with you for a bit. Barely anyone has just a mom and a dad and the kids."

"Lincoln does."

"But would you really want Lincoln as your son?"

She paused for a minute, looking at herself in the mirror, then burst out laughing, and her lip split open again.

"God you're so right," she said.

I sat on the edge of the tub and she came and sat next to me.

"Anyway, it doesn't matter," she said. "It would just suck is all, if I was actually gay …"

I'm still in this bathroom stall with my smudged thumb raised like I'm giving a thumbs up, and I've looked at my hand for so long it no longer seems like a part of my body.

A car alarm goes off somewhere in the distance, and realization comes down like rain from a clear blue sky.

Melissa is gay. She tried to tell me in Mark's backyard last week, but I was too annoyed with her to notice. Melissa is gay. That's what Lincoln was saying. That's the reason Dan broke up with her.

Everyone knows but me, and I'm the one who told them.

16

It takes all my willpower to walk to Melissa's street, but now that I'm here I don't know what to do. It's after midnight, and the only light is the orange-yellow glow from the side lamp in Melissa's bedroom. I blur my eyes and stare at the square of light in the dark house in the dark night like that little square of light is all there is.

My hands shake on my phone and I feel nervous like I've never been before.

"Yes," she says on the other end of the line. Her voice sounds odd and far away, not like she's just on the other side of a window.

"Are you … I'm outside your house. Can you come for a walk?"

She's wearing her brother's old jean jacket and the shoes she bought in May when her mom took us prom dress shopping in Toronto. And now we're both standing on the sidewalk staring at her house.

"I hope I didn't wake you up," I say.

"I was just finishing packing. I'm leaving tomorrow."

"Tomorrow," I echo.

A police car speeds down the highway with its sirens on, and we both turn toward the sound like we'll be able to see it.

"Where did you want to walk?" she asks. "Is this ... I mean, what is this about?"

But my mind goes blank. I had half prepared half a speech, but now that we're standing here my tongue is too big for my mouth and everything I was going to say sounds like something from an after-school special.

"It's your last night in Cavanaugh," I say, because apparently we didn't already establish that. "You decide."

She sighs, then starts walking fast out of our neighborhood with her back to me and her curly hair flapping behind her. I walk double speed to catch up, but there's something hard about the way Melissa moves through the streets that makes it impossible for me to speak.

We follow the road past our elementary school and the park toward the center of town. The blue light from a convenience store's neon Open sign reflects off Melissa's skin because nothing can touch her, not even me.

Melissa walks with her head down, stomping out her pace, and I follow a step or two behind like I'm chasing her. She switches directions and dodges down side streets and back alleys, and I am a stalker she's trying to get away from.

We don't stop until we get to the central overpass, and then we lean over the edge and stare down at the cars driving in straight lines to anywhere but here, red lights and yellow lights and none of them shining for us.

The wind hits against our faces and messes up our hair, and Melissa says something but I can't hear over the constant traffic that's been driving through us all our lives.

"What?" I ask.

"I didn't say anything."

"Okay." Only it's not. There's something enormous between us, and I feel like I've got too much blood. Everything seems to be happening all at once and I just want to grab hold of something and say stop, please, let me look at you before you're gone.

Finally I look at Melissa's face, the brown hair flying over her head and her eyes still on the traffic below, and I say, "You're gay, aren't you?"

She looks at me and chews her bottom lip, and the dimple on her chin gets dark.

"Congratulations," she says. "You're the last person on earth to know." And she starts walking again, even faster this time, still with something dark and unbreakable between us. I'm waiting for her to grow wings and lift from the earth.

There are things I'm supposed to be saying right now, about Melissa, about us, about what we were like when we were kids and who we are now, but Melissa is walking so fast I can barely catch my breath, and as each minute passes it's harder and harder to open my mouth.

Our footsteps get louder and the houses get farther apart. The paved road turns to gravel, and Melissa is a dark blur I'll never catch.

I don't know how my legs are moving anymore, and I don't know where we're going, down one gravel road and up another with the landscape on flashcards before us. It switches between forests and farms, forests and farms, and Melissa is running now and I run after her with my lungs red in my chest and my heart beating too loud.

— 169 —

Melissa looks back every few minutes to check if I'm still there, but I can't tell if she's doing it to reassure herself or to see if she's lost me yet.

We turn onto a dead end with a slope and a forest in front of us. I stumble and have to stop to catch my breath.

"Wait," I call. "Where are we even going? I think we should talk."

She stops and turns around, and her eyes are filled with that same electricity they had when she came to my house covered in dirt and blood last winter. Her chest is heaving, and she looks more like a horse than a girl.

I have to open and close my mouth a few times before I manage to get any words out.

"I should have realized," I start. "I should been there for you. I didn't mean to tell everyone." But my voice sounds odd and too small. It feels more like what I'm supposed to say than what I want to say, and Melissa has already turned her back to me and is heading toward the end of the road where the land dips down.

There's a wooden pole ahead stuck into the ground with two signs nailed to it. *Private Property,* says the first sign. *No Dumping,* says the one underneath, and Melissa's head disappears as she lowers herself down the slope to whatever is below.

I follow her to the edge and find a graveyard for all the things humans don't want anymore. There are shopping carts and bicycles, a whole car and ten or fifteen fridges and freezers. The clear early-September moonlight shines down on everything, and with the dark forest behind them these fridges look like they're glowing. It's like they're somehow still plugged in with their lightbulbs working, a dozen electric tombs chucked down a hill at the edge of a forest.

It's the moonlight and the fridges and Melissa climbing down the hill toward them and our whole last summer that's already over, and all of it suddenly makes me feel so guilty for all the time I've wasted.

The grass is wet with dew, and Melissa slips and slides down the hill. She lands with a loud thump and her foot jammed against a refrigerator.

"Fuck," I hear from the bottom of the hill.

"Are you okay?"

She lies there for a minute twisting her foot one way and then the other like a broken doll.

I sit on my bum to slide down the wet grass and land almost on top of her.

"Is it broken?" I ask. She's taken her shoe off and holds her ankle while she twists her foot.

"I think it's okay," she says, and we lie still, feeling the wet grass seep through our clothes and the cold stars against our skin. All around us are all the things humans thought they wanted only now they don't.

Melissa picks up a rusting can opener and spins the handle. It makes a terrible squeaking sound that rings out over the refrigerators and the forests and the fields as though it's the sound the whole old earth is making as it spins around the sun again and again.

And then she takes the can opener and chucks it as far into the pit as she can.

It lands with a pinging sound and she finally turns to me and says, "We're totally going to get Cat-AIDS down here."

"It's okay, I'm already infected."

"Me, too," she says.

The slope we slid down is too steep for Melissa's twisted ankle, so we take the long way out. She supports herself on my shoulder as we make the slow trek around the field of abandoned refrigerators, over a fence and through a farmer's field.

When we get back to the gravel road, we stand looking at each other in the moonlight. I pull a leaf out of Melissa's hair and she puts her hand on my cheek. Her skin is cold and soft.

And then she slaps me, hard.

I stagger back tasting metal and the moonlight like my mouth is full of gold teeth and this is a dream about eating trains all over again.

"Shit," I say.

"You deserve it," she says.

"I know."

The walk back into town in one way seems endless and in another seems like no time at all. The whole way Melissa limps, leaning against my shoulder with my arm around her waist. We pass the fields we only saw in flashes when we were running, now covered in dew and moonlight like the entire earth is precious and rare and the most beautiful place we've ever been.

When we get to the overpass we look out at the cars again with our hands cold in our pockets and the wind cold on our ears, and I somehow find myself telling Melissa about Tyler, about lying to him and how when he confronted me in the park I didn't know what to say.

The cars go by below like they always do, a line of yellow headlights and a line of red taillights and the blackness they disappear into.

"You know, sometimes you just have to be brave," Melissa says, staring at the road with the wind in her hair. "I've got a plan for when I go to school tomorrow. It's all new people who won't know anything about me, and I'm just going to start off telling them I'm gay like it's no big deal." She presses her fingers to the concrete barrier to hold herself steady and nods as though she's rehearsing the words she's going to say the next day.

"Maybe you just have to go to Tyler and tell him the truth," she says. "Say, this is who I am and this is why I lied, and hope that he accepts you."

"And if he doesn't?" I ask.

Melissa's fingers are white on the barrier. All the cuts from where she punched concrete two weeks ago have healed over. Her skin is brand new and she's about to be released into the world all over again.

"He will," she says. "He has to, right? They have to." She lets go of the barrier and examines where the rough stone left pockmarks in her fingertips.

A car on the highway swerves from one lane into another. The car behind it honks, and they carry on into the blackness.

"I don't know," I say, watching her make a fist and release it again and again. "It's not like the movies where I apologize to Tyler and tell him what happened and we automatically go back to the way we were, or you tell people at school you're gay and you're suddenly not scared or angry or messed up all the time."

Her hand is in a fist again. She rolls her knuckles back and forth across the concrete barrier, then leans against it and spits over the edge.

"You're right," she tells me. "But nothing will happen if we don't try. We might as well go out into the world and do our best."

That night at Neil's party, I remember telling Tyler about the highway that cuts the town in two. I told him how everyone thinks if they follow it they'll find somewhere better. All my friends who are leaving will probably end up getting jobs and getting married, buying houses and having babies, but at least they'll know what's out there.

Melissa's body is warm beside mine, and her hair blows into my face. She doesn't know who she is or what she wants, either, but at least she's trying. Maybe Lincoln will hate Australia and come back in a month or two, but he's trying, too.

We stop on the sidewalk outside Melissa's house and look at her front door and then look at each other. She has her bottom lip in her mouth again, and she leans to the side, putting weight on her good leg.

"I was so pissed off at you this summer," I tell her, and she runs her fingers through her hair.

"I know," she says. "It was stupid. I just … I had all these weird feelings, and …" The way she's looking at her shoes, she could be eight years old.

All I want to do is wrap my arms around her, feed her chocolate chip cookies and never let anything bad happen to her again.

"It was … I don't know what it was," she says. A piece of hair falls in front of her face and I move it behind her ear.

She looks up at me, puts her hand to my cheek and smiles.

"I hope I didn't hit you too hard," she says.

"Just hard enough."

"Good." And she pats the tender skin and then kisses my other cheek.

I watch her walk back toward her house. Her brown hair is a halo above her head, and the way she swaggers it's hard to believe that she is another person who doesn't know who she is or what she wants.

And when Melissa gets to her door she throws me a peace sign, two fingers in the air. She spits over her porch railing, then disappears into the house.

17

The bell on the pawnshop door rings as I enter, and all the things once owned by someone else and ready to be adopted again reach out to me. I keep my eyes down and walk along the aisle, but when I get to the counter it's not Tyler but an older man who would look exactly like Tyler if Tyler was carved out of meat.

"Well, hello there," he says. There's kindness in his voice, even as he eyes me up and down.

When I open my mouth the first time nothing but sand pours out, but eventually I find my tongue and manage to tell him I'm looking for Tyler.

"He should be out back somewhere," the man says.

The laneway beside the pawnshop is empty and so is the alley that runs behind the buildings, and maybe Tyler's uncle wouldn't tell Tyler a girl came in looking for him or maybe he would, and Tyler would know that I was here and that I chickened out.

The fire-escape railing is cold, and I grip it so hard that the metal bites into my skin.

Melissa must be landing in Halifax by now. Her plane took off at noon, and in an hour or two she'll be meeting people she might be friends with for the rest of her life. She'll be trying to sound casual as she tells them she's gay and waits to hear how they respond.

The staircase is too short, and I'm already at the top of it, staring at Tyler's back in a lawn chair. His hair is out of its ponytail and blowing in the wind.

My shoes crunch on the gravel roof, and Tyler turns to watch me walk toward him.

"Hey," I say.

He doesn't move from his chair, so I come around in front of him. I can feel each of my teeth in my mouth and every one of my organs moving in a different direction.

"Is it okay if I sit?" I ask, but I'm having a hard time controlling my body and I've already landed in a chair by the time Tyler says, "Yeah, I guess."

"I don't know if it'll mean much now," I say. "But I came to apologize."

Our chairs face away from Cavanaugh toward fields and forests and towns I've driven through without ever looking up to notice that there are people there trying their best to be happy.

Even though it's daytime now and Melissa is in Halifax and I am on a roof, I feel like a little part of both of us is still wandering those fields, and another part is on a bridge overlooking the highway, and Melissa is telling me again and again how I have to be brave.

"I guess what it is, is this," I begin, only I don't know where to start. I don't think I've ever actually told this story before. Everyone just somehow already knows.

"I guess my mother was always sick," I start again, and Tyler looks over at me with his eyebrows climbing his forehead.

"Do you know this part?" I ask. "Is this what your aunt told you?"

He shakes his head and cracks his knuckles.

"Shit," I say. I prop my feet on a milk crate in front of me, but the milk crate is too high or my chair is too low or my limbs are too loose.

"She had depression and other things," I say. "And when I was three things got real bad."

Tyler shifts in his chair with his eyes still on his knuckles.

"We were living in Alberta, and we drove all day and all night back to Cavanaugh." I kick the milk crate away and bring my knees into my chest. "I remember her face glowing yellow and then going dark as we passed under the streetlights over and over again. And then when we got here we checked into a shitty motel at the edge of town, and it was like everything just stopped."

Tyler looks up from his hands and our eyes meet. The whole earth is quiet for a fraction of a second until he looks away again.

"I don't know how long we were there for. A few days or maybe a week," I say. I cross my ankles and wrap my arms around my knees like I'm trying to tie myself into an unbreakable knot.

My lungs feel like they're made of cardboard and I'm not sure how I'll survive the rest of this, but then I think of my dad and me driving to Montreal when I was ten even though there was no one there to meet. We packed the car the night before we left, and when my dad closed the trunk he turned to me and said, "Well, Emily, the show must go on." And then he started laughing. It was this loud and panicked half-crazed laugh that went on and on until I started laughing, too, and we were both in hysterics in the driveway for no reason at all …

I lace my fingers together and begin again. "And then one night, my mother went into the bathroom and … and she killed herself."

The wind picks up and there's a high-pitched ringing in my ears. I tie my limbs tighter, and I wait for Tyler to speak.

He tries to crack his knuckles again but no sound comes out. He pushes his hair behind his ears and squints at the fields spread out below us like he's willing himself to be magically transported there or really anywhere that isn't beside me and this thing that I've been stained with.

"So that's the story," I say. "It just seems like my whole life I've only ever been seen as the little kid who was left alone to find her mother's body in some shitty motel bathroom at the edge of town."

Tyler breathes out hard and a flock of Canada geese flies overhead. They're honking loud and panicked like they lost track of time and should have headed south for winter weeks ago.

"And then I met you," I say. "And you didn't know, and I thought I could just … I wanted you to see me for me."

Tyler shifts in his chair and bites on the knuckle of his index finger.

"It's not an excuse," I tell him. "I shouldn't have lied, and I'm sorry I hurt you. I … it was selfish." I slowly begin untangling myself, feeling the blood rush into my limbs and the ache that comes with it.

I walk to the edge of the roof to look at where the building falls away. When I look back at Tyler he's still staring past me, and I know that if I leapt from the roof right now, I wouldn't fly. Instead I sit at the edge with the gravel digging into my butt and my feet swinging into the empty space, and I ask myself if I feel different, if I'm a different person than I was when I met Tyler two weeks ago.

A car drives fast down a country road away from Cavanaugh, and the gravel shifts behind me. It's Tyler's footsteps, but I don't turn to see if he's walking toward me or away until there's motion in the corner of my eye, and he sits beside me at the edge.

"I don't know what to say," he tells me, and I tell him that's okay.

"It happened a long time ago, and I've dealt with it. Now I just want to try to be happy and have a nice life."

"That sounds like a really good idea," Tyler says. He picks up a piece of gravel and we stare at it in his palm.

"No more lies," I say. "You don't have to forgive me or anything. But I really am sorry."

Tyler nods and closes his fingers around the rock. When he opens his hand again, I half expect the rock to have turned into a butterfly, but it's still just a rock picked out from a pile of a thousand other rocks.

We both stare out at the forests and the fields at the edge of Cavanaugh but also at the edge of the rest of the world, every road leading to another road, and every street in North America and South America connecting to every other street. I bet if you tried hard enough, you could find a way to get to every place on the entire planet.

Tyler takes the rock he's been holding and puts it in my hand.

It's warm and hard, and its jagged edge bites into my palm.

18

I take Tyler's hand and press it to the wallpaper in my grandma's front hallway. It's Braille, and it's supposed to tell him all the things I can't.

His hand is warm in mine, and when he looks at me he smiles to show his crooked teeth, but his eyes are a snowman's button eyes on the first warm day in March.

"I lived here from when I was three until I was seven," I begin. "I broke my arm jumping off these stairs one time, and that stain on the carpet is from where I spilled paint."

I watch Tyler's face while I tell him everything that's ever happened to me. How my grandma used to let me cut my hair myself. How for two weeks when I was six we had a pet field mouse we fed peanut butter sandwiches to. Tyler nods along and his skin is warm and smooth against mine, but there's a whirring in my chest like a fan with loose blades because maybe this is too much for him.

"We used to pretend to speak German," I say. "And when I was five our washing machine broke. I took baths with the dirty clothes while my grandma tried to wash everything all at once."

I lead Tyler from the hallway to the living room, and he squints at the bright sun coming through the open windows. Once his eyes adjust, I watch them roam from the old rolls of wallpaper to the upside-down flowerpots to the men's dress shoes scattered around the room.

My grandma is making lunch for us in the kitchen, and I move an empty egg carton, two burnt-out lightbulbs and a framed picture of a coral reef from the couch so that we have enough room to sit.

"I'm a little worried about this lunch," I whisper to Tyler.

"Why? What's wrong?" He picks up a teacup in the shape of a rabbit doing a headstand and examines the top-hat-shaped saucer underneath.

"Once when I was seven, right before I moved in with my dad, my grandma made me pretend that we were cats. All we ate was cat food for two full days." I glance over at him and make a face like I'm shocked by my own confession.

Tyler laughs, but the room is suddenly too hot.

"That's gross," he says. He sets the teacup on top of a transistor radio and picks up a plastic horse figurine.

"I know, but I was seven. I didn't really have a choice."

Tyler looks up from the horse and blinks.

"Oh," he says. "Right." And he makes the horse gallop across the arm of the couch.

"When I was nine, I refused to eat anything but mayonnaise, onion and peanut butter sandwiches," he tells me.

And now it's my turn to laugh.

"What?" I ask. "How did you even come up with that?"

"I know. I thought I was some master chef or something."

Luckily my grandma comes through with a relatively normal meal. It's ham-and-cheese sandwiches and apple slices. The only weird thing is that the apple slices are submerged in a bowl of water like drowning half-moons.

"I didn't want the apples to go brown," my grandma explains. She balances the bowl on top of an empty binocular case on the coffee table.

"That's actually really smart," says Tyler.

We eat our sandwiches and talk about the weather and what classes Tyler is taking in night school, and later my grandma brings in tea and cookies that taste like they were baked a few decades ago.

"Oh, I forgot to tell you," I say while I'm waiting for my tea to cool. "I'm going to Montreal next week with my dad."

"What for?" asks Tyler. He takes a bite of his cookie, pulls back and slowly lowers it to his napkin.

"I'm just going to see what it's like and to maybe check out one of the culinary schools there." I balance my teacup on the edge of the coffee table and lean back on the couch against a pair of acid-washed jeans. "I'll make sure to ask the teachers about mayo and peanut butter sandwiches."

"And serving apple slices in bowls of water," Tyler adds.

"I wouldn't want to give away too much, though," I say. "These are million-dollar ideas. Someone might try to steal them for their own restaurant."

We all nod and I shift on the couch, trying to pull the jeans from behind my back to stop the zipper from eating me.

"I was thinking maybe one day we could go to Toronto to-gether, too," I say to Tyler with my eyes down, winding the legs of the jeans around and around my arm.

"You were, were you?"

I glance over at him, and a lopsided smile slides up his face.

"You might as well show me what's so great about it and why you want to leave *Cavanaugh, Canada's Armpit*, as soon as possible."

"Well, now," my grandma says, spilling a drip of tea on her shirt. "Cavanaugh's a lovely town." She puts her cup back on the coffee table and examines the tea on her shirt but leaves it to air-dry.

"I know, Grandma, but I guess I should see what's out there."

My grandma still looks concerned.

"Maybe you can come," I tell her, unwinding the jeans from my arm and throwing them behind me. "The three of us could get a condo downtown and go to all the hip clubs."

My grandma looks between Tyler and me for a second, as though she's actually considering it. And then she laughs, and her laugh is as loud as a man's.

Tyler and I are gathering our things and just about to leave when my grandma waves her hands in front of us like an amateur magician.

"I almost forgot," she says. "I have something for you, Emily." She goes to the bookshelf by the window and comes back with a square box made of cardboard. One of its corners is dented from its trips across town in the bottom of my bag.

"It's so strange. I could have sworn I gave these to you weeks ago, but I found them in your old bedroom earlier today." She sets the box on my lap and smiles to show her dentures. "Or maybe I had two sets of teeth."

She sits beside me on the couch. My grandma on one side and Tyler on the other, and my head swivels between them.

I take a deep breath and pretend to be surprised to see six gold-capped teeth on a folded-up tissue.

"Wow, Grandma," I say. "Thanks."

Tyler shifts beside me, but he seems surprisingly calm.

I wince as my grandma holds up one of the stained and broken teeth to examine it, but then Tyler takes the box from me to stare at its contents, and suddenly all three of us are sitting on my grandma's couch inspecting her old teeth like it's a totally normal thing to do. We look over the ridges and the roots and where the gold was joined to the bone.

"You know," I say. "I heard somewhere that gold is a heavy element. All the gold that was on the planet when the earth was made sank to the center when the earth cooled down. All the gold we find now came down from outer space millions of years later."

Tyler and my grandma both look at me, and for a second the room feels too hot again. I look from the tooth in my grandma's hand to the rest of the teeth crowded together on the folded tissue.

"I don't know if that's true," says Tyler, handing the box back.

"It could be," says my grandma. "I've lived for seventy-five years now, and the world still surprises me every day." She closes her hand around the tooth and puts her other hand on top of mine.

"Apparently there was a meteor shower years and years ago," I say. "And all the gold that we have is actually from shooting stars."

Tyler looks between my grandma and me, and I hold up a tooth in the light from the open window.

"It could be true," he says.

"I hope it is," I tell him.

Outside, two kids on bicycles ride down the street. They're shouting and they're laughing, and I imagine the gold in this tooth coming down as a shooting star from outer space, drawing a yellow line of light across the sky.

Tyler smiles and my grandma smiles, and somewhere down the street a dog barks and a car drives by. If we sit still and listen very carefully, we can hear the faint hum of the highway in the distance, too, traffic like waves washing against the shore. It's one road connecting to all the other roads, and cars are driving all day and all night. They're driving to all the places I've never been, and all the places I might one day go.

Acknowledgments

Thank you to my family, especially my parents Nancy and Rick and my brothers Benjamin and Sean, for their endless encouragement and inspiration to be myself, think differently and pursue my dreams.

Thank you to my editor Shelley Tanaka for finding merit in a very different draft of this book and helping to transform it into what it is today.

Thank you to Janice Zawerbny for helping this book find a home, and thank you to all the fabulous people at Groundwood Books and House of Anansi for believing in this book and the power of books in general.

Thank you to The Super Best Friend Society, especially Amber Wareham, Jess Braun and Rachel Klein, for reading countless awful drafts of this novel far before it was ready for human eyes.

Thank you to Patrick Plestid, Jess Taylor and my professors in Creative Writing at York University.

Thank you to Gwen Barton for the gold teeth.

Thank you to Gwen Cumyn and Laurel Terrio for the tea, friendship and endless pep talks.

Thank you to Alan Cumyn for the advice.

Thank you to Broken Social Scene.

Thank you to Emily Sehl, Meaghan Carey, my Beechwood Family, and Meghan, Sharron and Cherise at RTI. All of you have been my constant cheerleaders.

Thank you to the countless other people in Toronto, Edinburgh and throughout the world who read early drafts of this book and listened to me go on about it for the past six years. I couldn't have done it without your support and encouragement.

JANE OZKOWSKI has a BA in English and Creative Writing from York University. She worked in the office at a motorcycle driving school for many years, and although she does not have a motorcycle, she does have her license in case she needs to make a quick getaway. *Watching Traffic* is her first novel.

Jane is the winner of House of Anansi's Broken Social Scene Story Contest, and she is currently working on an adult novel set during the apocalypse. She lives in Toronto.